camp CONFIDENTIAL
Super Special!

Reunion

GROSSET & DUNLAP
Published by the Penguin Group
Penguin Group (USA) Inc., 375 Hudson Street, New York,
New York 10014, USA
Penguin Group (Canada), 90 Eglinton Avenue East, Suite 700, Toronto, Ontario
M4P 2Y3, Canada (a division of Pearson Penguin Canada Inc.)
Penguin Books Ltd., 80 Strand, London WC2R 0RL, England
Penguin Group Ireland, 25 St. Stephen's Green, Dublin 2, Ireland
(a division of Penguin Books Ltd.)
Penguin Group (Australia), 250 Camberwell Road, Camberwell, Victoria 3124,
Australia (a division of Pearson Australia Group Pty. Ltd.)
Penguin Books India Pvt. Ltd., 11 Community Centre, Panchsheel Park,
New Delhi—110 017, India
Penguin Group (NZ), 67 Apollo Drive, Rosedale, North Shore 0632,
New Zealand (a division of Pearson New Zealand Ltd.)
Penguin Books (South Africa) (Pty.) Ltd., 24 Sturdee Avenue,
Rosebank, Johannesburg 2196, South Africa

Penguin Books Ltd., Registered Offices: 80 Strand, London WC2R 0RL, England

If you purchased this book without a cover, you should be aware that this book
is stolen property. It was reported as "unsold and destroyed" to the publisher,
and neither the author nor the publisher has received any payment for this
"stripped book."

The scanning, uploading, and distribution of this book via the Internet or
via any other means without the permission of the publisher is illegal and
punishable by law. Please purchase only authorized electronic editions, and do
not participate in or encourage electronic piracy of copyrighted materials. Your
support of the author's rights is appreciated.

Cover design by Ching N. Chan
Front cover images © Image Source Photography /Veer Incorporated

Text copyright © 2009 by Grosset & Dunlap. All rights reserved. Published
by Grosset & Dunlap, a division of Penguin Young Readers Group, 345 Hudson
Street, New York, New York 10014. GROSSET & DUNLAP is a trademark of
Penguin Group (USA) Inc. Printed in the U.S.A.

Library of Congress Control Number: 2008054002

ISBN 978-0-448-45187-9   10 9 8 7 6 5 4 3 2 1

camp CONFIDENTIAL
Super Special!

Reunion

by Melissa J. Morgan

Grosset & Dunlap

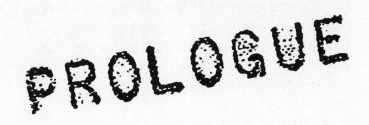

PROLOGUE

From: NatalieNYC
To: Aries8
Subject: Summer blues!

Hey Jenna,

Greetings from the Big Apple! How are you?

I'm trying to keep busy now that we don't have a summer at Lakeview to look forward to. In case you were wondering exactly how desperate the situation is, Dad even convinced me to sign up for some improv classes through a performing arts school here in the city. (There may or may not have been a shopping-related bribe involved.) I know—you can't picture it. I tried to convince him that acting is *so* not my thing, but I think he gets excited about me possibly following in his footsteps. Anyway, maybe now I'll be able to compare notes with Brynn the next time I see her. She'll be so excited to have another "thespian" (her word, of course) among our campmates! Speaking of . . . do you know what she's doing this summer, now that Lakeview's shut down? Have you heard from anyone else? And what about you, by the way? Inquiring minds want to know! Tell me I'm not the only one who is feeling kinda lost without camp.

Write back soon and give me all the gossip.

Miss you,
Nat

From: Aries8
To: NatalieNYC
Subject: Re: Summer blues!

Hiya, city slicker!

I'm glad to hear that you're keeping busy. (But I would *so* pay money to watch you in an improv class! LOL! I hope the shopping spree was at least worth it!) I am, too. My community center has a summer soccer clinic that I'll go to three times a week, and on the off days I'll play tennis with Adam. Naturally, I plan to kick his butt 100 percent of the time. We may be twins, but when it comes to athletic ability, all Blooms are not created equal!

I got an e-mail from Brynn a few weeks ago, and it sounds like she's planning to do some kind of arts program in her town. I think she's disappointed. She expected it to be a huge dose of high-falutin' *theatre*, but when she went to the orientation, she found out that instead it's some hippie teacher encouraging her to "engage her body in creative movement." Like, I think it's mostly interpretive dance or something. I told her a little interpretive dance never hurt anybody (as far as I know). I'm not sure that she was totally convinced.

Oh well. I wish we could see each other at Lakeview again, but it looks like that's not in the cards anymore. At least we've all found *some* way to spend the summer vacation. For better or for worse . . .

Write back soon!

—Jenna

"I love the Film Forum," Natalie sighed, stepping off the elevator and into the plush hallway of her apartment building. "Where else can you see a movie like *The Wizard of Oz* on the big screen?" She reached into her quilted pink tote bag and fished out a jangly silver keychain, unlocking the door to the Manhattan apartment she shared with her mother.

"Also, they have the best popcorn in the city," her best friend Hannah replied. "What do you think they put in it to make it so extra yummy?"

The two girls crossed through the spacious living room and back toward Natalie's pristine bedroom. As usual, her mother was still out, working all hours like the crazed professional that she was. Not that Natalie minded having freedom; she knew she was way lucky that her parental supervision was mostly kept to a minimum, unlike some of her friends, who had all kinds of curfews and rules and things like that.

Rules. Natalie shuddered just thinking about it. Rules probably involved not being allowed to go downtown in a cab with your BFF to watch a movie in an awesome art-house theater.

"Earth to Natalie," Hannah chimed in. "Do you not have an opinion on the great popcorn mystery?"

Natalie shrugged, settling onto her plush bed with her sleek laptop. "As long as it's so delectable, why ask questions?"

"Fair enough," Hannah agreed, collapsing next to her in a heap on the bed. "So," she continued, propping herself up on one elbow, "now that you've seen that movie a million *and one* times, be honest—does the Cowardly Lion still freak you out?"

Nat made a face. "What can I say? His voice is so thick and creepy. But after seeing the movie a million *and one* times, I think I can handle it, finally. The one that really impresses me is Judy Garland. I mean, she can cry on command. That's *acting!* She totally knows how to 'go there.' I think 'going there' is going to play a key role in my improv classes this summer."

"Go where?" Hannah looked puzzled, even through her toothy grin.

Natalie rolled her eyes. "I think it's an

expression. At least, I *hope* it's an expression. The only place I want to go is Pinkberry after class every week. Seriously—I don't know if I'm cut out to be an actress. That's, like, my dad's thing, or Brynn's." Natalie's father was the movie star Tad Maxwell, who had appeared in a bunch of blockbuster spy movies that were immensely popular. And Brynn was Natalie's friend from summer camp who had a flair for the dramatic.

Natalie could be plenty dramatic herself when she wanted to be. But that didn't mean she had designs on seeing her name in lights. She was happy to leave that to her friends and her father.

"I think it's cute that your dad wants a little mini-me," Hannah insisted. "He's all showing he cares and stuff. It's sweet."

"Great. Then *you* 'go there,'" Nat countered. She smiled to show she was teasing. Mostly. "Honestly, Han? I never in a million years thought I would say this, but I'm so bummed that Camp Lakeview closed. I really miss it, and all of my camp friends. And you're going to be jetting off to France for your dad's sabbatical, so it's going to be superlonely around here."

"I could stash you in my suitcase; you could stow away," Hannah offered. "We could spend all summer sunning on the Riviera!"

Natalie raised an eyebrow. "Are you trying to make me feel worse? You know I have a fear of small, enclosed spaces. So your suitcase—and hence, France—are out. Pfft." She sighed. "No France, no

Lakeview . . . just a summer of doing breathing exercises and pantomime and stuff . . ." She let her voice trail off forlornly and flipped open her laptop, tapping away at the keyboard, firing it up, and scanning her e-mails.

"This from the girl who always claimed to be allergic to nature," Hannah said, shaking her head in disbelief. "I am shocked. Shocked, I tell you."

But Natalie wasn't listening to Hannah anymore; she was too caught up in what she was reading onscreen. Suddenly she sat up straight. "You're not the only one! Check out the e-mail that I just got!" She flipped her computer around so that Hannah could see the screen clearly.

"Blah blah Dr. Steve—he's the Lakeview director, right?" Hannah asked, scanning the screen.

Natalie nodded excitedly. "Yep. Well, he was, until Lakeview closed. But keep reading!" She jabbed her index finger back in the direction of the computer.

"Camp Walla Walla?" Hannah read aloud. "In Connecticut?"

Natalie nearly bounced off the bed and onto the floor, she was so hyped up. She looked at Hannah, her eyes shining with enthusiasm. "Camp Walla Walla," she repeated, "in Connecticut. Dr. Steve made a last-minute decision to work there this summer!" She paused, giving the information a moment to sink in. "And he wants us to join him!"

"Maybe you got your wish," Hannah said,

looking pleased for her friend. "You could be going back to camp after all!"

Posted by: Jenna
Subject: Walla Walla—who's in?

Hey guys!
Can you believe the e-mail from Dr. Steve about Camp Walla Walla? I know I can't! Don't get me wrong—I was getting psyched for soccer and tennis (I mean, you guys know me), but now that Dr. Steve's got a new camp, I'm thinking we Lakeview girls need to start a new tradition!

I did some Googling on Camp Walla Walla, and it looks *amazing*! They've got a top-of-the-line ropes course, archery, an Olympic-sized pool *and* a lake, and a *serious* boating and outdoor survival program. It sounds totally cool and rustic and outdoorsy, just up my alley.

Oh, and did I mention the thing where it's also *amazing*?

Who's in?

Posted by: Priya
Subject: Here's to new traditions!

Um, so I'm no Olympic archer, and I'm kind of afraid of heights, but it's hard not to get psyched about Walla Walla with your whole ringing endorsement, J!

Posted by: Jenna
Subject: Totally psyched!

Because of the amazingness, right? Come on, girls! We *have* to go. Lakeview reunited! The gang's all here! Best friends forever!

Posted by: Brynn
Subject: Dramarama

OMG, Jen, we get it. And they say *I'm* the dramatic one. Hmph. Do they do any plays or anything, or are we just going to be learning to identify poisonous berries and how to make a sleep shelter from a bikini top and stuff?

Posted by: Jenna
Subject: Aww c'mon . . .

If you come to camp, Brynn, I swear I'll run lines with you every night. And you can borrow my bathing suit for your sleep shelter, if it comes to that.

Posted by: Chelsea
Subject: I'm in!

I'll go if you guys go. I think my parents were worried that I was just going to be bumming around the house all summer, anyway. They'll be relieved for me to get outside and into the great outdoors and stuff.

Posted by: Sloan
Subject: Me too!

Count me in. Arizona gets crazy-hot in the summertime, and anyway, my tarot cards say that there is a blessing to be found in nature. And everyone knows the cards don't lie.

Posted by: Jenna
Subject: Halfway there . . .

Woo-hoo! That's three of us! Priya? Brynn? Nat? I know you're out there! Quit lurking and get with the program!

Posted by: Priya
Subject: !!!

All right, all right, just stop with the exclamation points! It's like you're shouting at me across cyber-space. My parents say I can come. And I'll do you one better: Jordan and David are going to come, too! Aren't you glad my best friend is a guy? I bring the cute boys with me wherever I go.

Posted by: Jenna
Subject: Yoo-hoo?!

It's down to Nat and Brynn. You're the last holdouts. What's it going to be?

Posted by: Natalie
Subject: Count me in.

You're lucky that you caught me during a weak moment. I'll come, especially if it means I can escape torturous improv class. I think week one is an exercise in channeling our pets. Do I seem like the sort of person who would want to channel her pet (if I had one!)? I refuse to unleash my inner hamster.

I'm not gonna lie, though, Jenna—I'm a little worried about the whole sports theme you're so hyped up on.

Posted by: Jenna
Subject: Do Not Fear the Sports!

NATALIE! I will take your turn in dodgeball for you! I will run relays in your place! I will score endless free throws in Horse in your name.

Posted by: Natalie
Subject: Surprise

<giggle>
All right, all right. That sounds okay. As long as you swear I won't have to break a sweat (or a nail) if I don't want to.

Annnddddd . . . here's a surprise for you guys: I talked Reed into coming to camp, too! He said he was going to try to spend the summer holed up in his father's screening room, but honestly, I think he liked the idea

of camp and other kids his age. And now that there's no
Logan in the picture anymore, maybe Reed and I can pick
up where we left off with our crushing!

Posted by: Jenna
Subject: Yay!

Silly Nat—I should have known you'd be in if there
were cute boys involved. Not that I'm complaining! Yay
for cute boys! Yay for Walla Walla! Yay for *us*!

Posted by: Brynn
Subject: ???

Reed's coming? No way am I missing out on
Natalie's L.A. boy. I'm in!

Posted by: Natalie
Subject: Double yay!

I never thought I'd feel this way, but hear, hear!
We're going back to camp!

chapter

ONE

"Oh. My. *Wow.*"

Jenna Bloom looked up from her duffel bags to find her friend and fellow Camp Lakeview exile, Natalie Goode, staring at her like she'd just sprouted a second head. She was totally psyched to see Nat, of course—it'd been, like, a whole summer since they'd last hung out—but was suddenly concerned that her face was streaked with leftover strawberry yogurt from lunchtime or something equally icky.

"What?" she asked, bringing a hand to her cheek self-consciously. "Do I—"

"Your *hair!*" Natalie shrieked, rushing forward to run her fingers through Jenna's newly glossy, stick-straight locks. "What did you *do?*"

Jenna winced. Natalie's voice had reached an octave generally reserved for dogs or other members of the animal kingdom.

"Oh, yeah," she said. She reached up and flipped her light brown hair off of one shoulder, remembering. "I got, um, one of those straight perms? For Stephanie's sweet sixteen? Stephanie thought it would look cool?

And, you know, I never ever change my hair, so I thought maybe it was time?"

Her uptalking betrayed the fact that Jenna was a tomboy by nature, way more into layups than lip gloss. Natalie was the resident camp glamourista. But the truth was, Jenna was kind of into her shiny, shiny hair, and was glad that her older sister had suggested it. Maybe all those summers at Lakeview with Nat had finally rubbed off on her. It was at Lakeview that she'd met her first boyfriend, after all. And they'd even agreed to stay together after Lakeview shut down. But during the school year, they ended up deciding they were better off as friends. Yes, her relationship with David was officially Of The Past . . . and so, unfortunately, was Camp Lakeview. Jenna and Natalie were about to take the plunge—or rather, the chartered coach bus—to the wild outskirts of Connecticut, to Camp Walla Walla, hence the duffel bags.

Jenna's eyes wandered down to Natalie's luggage. The girl had managed to drag not one but *two* enormous polka-dotted lavender bags *and* a hot pink trunk that could have doubled as a traffic sign. A very girly traffic sign.

"I see some things haven't changed," she said wryly. Natalie had never really been one for "roughing it."

"Hey!" Nat protested. "I love your hair. I also love my velour track suits. Leave my packing skills out of it." She grinned. "Seriously, though. What's the story here?" She glanced around at the chaos of the bus stop: piles of bags, backpacks, and trunks; older girls squealing and hugging as they reunited; younger first-timers looking nervous and watery-eyed as their parents patted them on the shoulders and directed them toward the bus. Nat and Jenna had agreed to be bus buddies for the ride from the North Jersey metro park up to Camp Walla Walla, and for her part, Jenna was gladder than ever that they had. She wasn't shy by nature, and she was *way* excited to check out Walla Walla and its extensive sports program, but Camp Lakeview had been . . . home. Theirs. And even though she and Nat would be meeting a group of friends at camp, well, now? Now they'd be the newbies.

She wasn't used to being a newbie.

"Uh, I think we have to put our luggage over in that pile—" she gestured limply at some chaos happening off in a far and dusty corner— "and then you have to tell some person with a clipboard that you're here. I already did that."

Natalie nodded. "Right. What is it with camps and clipboards? Remember how Dr. Steve used to wear one around his neck? Okay," Natalie said, breaking into Jenna's thoughts. "You're making a face. Clearly I've upset you with my fond memories of Dr. Steve's dorkier moments."

Jenna smiled weakly. "No, it's not that," she insisted. "I guess . . . it just kind of hit me. About camp. Like, how we're going somewhere new."

"Yeah, I kind of thought that was the idea when you e-mailed the bunk and said, 'Hey, what if we all go somewhere *new?'"* Nat's eyes twinkled so Jenna knew that she was teasing.

"You're funny," Jenna replied. "But, yeah. I'm just a little more freaked than I expected to be at the whole change of scenery thing. What if—I don't know? What if the girls at Walla Walla don't like to do *Seventeen* magazine quizzes before lights-out? What if the kayaks are moldy? What if they play soccer in some weird new way, like with croquet mallets or something—"

"Okay, you need to calm down, *stat,*" Natalie said, grabbing Jenna's wrists and swinging enthusiastically. "Have you forgotten one very important fact?"

Jenna eyed Natalie doubtfully.

"We're *us!*" Nat chirped, enthusiastic as ever. "The Lakeview girls! We rock and we *always* have one another's backs! This is going to be our best summer *ever.* For reals."

Jenna was quiet.

"Plus, you look fantastic, so this is the perfect time for a new beginning. And never mind that they *obviously* don't play soccer with croquet mallets since the mallets would *totally* snap in half with the awesome power of your Sporty Spice strength."

Jenna had to laugh at that.

"Better," Nat said. "Smiling is better. Now, should I assume that you have already scoped out the bus and saved us the best seats, exactly two-thirds of the way back?"

Jenna nodded. "That was the first thing I did. Well, second. After the part with the clipboard."

"Fabs," Natalie said. "I'll go check in and drop off my luggage. Then we can go brush up on our magazine quizzing. I came prepared." She tipped open the lip of her shoulder bag to reveal a dizzying array of colorful pages. Then her expression turned more serious.

"I mean it, Jenna," she said, her brown eyes sparkling. "Forget about being new. Not *only* are we going to have an amazing time, but I'd even bet you my favorite purple glitter nail polish that it's only a matter of time before the Lakeview girls *rule* Camp Walla Walla. Swearsies."

Jenna giggled again. It was hard to argue with Natalie when she was being all defiant and stuff. And if she was willing to put her purple glitter nail polish on the line, she was *definitely* not joking around.

So instead of arguing, Jenna just decided to cross her fingers and hope like heck that her friend was right. As far as plans went, it was solid enough. She scampered after Natalie, who was heading up the stairs and onto the bus. "Wait—" she called. "Do you have *Twist* in there?"

▲ ▲ ▲

Brynn was bouncing off the walls. She'd been the first to arrive at Camp Walla Walla, and, after staking claim to the only single bunk in the Oak tent (all of the tents at Walla Walla were named after trees. Also, they were tents, not bunks or cabins. So that was . . . new), she had spent about three hours pretending to flip through a paperback romance while waiting for her friends from Lakeview to *finally* show up.

They were taking forever. Which was, on the one hand, okay, since Brynn needed the time to prepare a little pep talk for Natalie, who was *definitely* going to freak out when she saw the tents. For Natalie, "roughing it" usually meant eating her sushi on a paper plate.

On the other hand, she was bursting with excitement to see her friends again. Where *were* they?

She glanced at her waterproof sports watch for what felt like the zillionth time, relieved to see that the big hand was creeping toward the three at long last. Jenna and Natalie's bus was supposed to be getting in at three, and Brynn was ready to give them the grand tour. Chelsea was already in the Oak tent, furiously unpacking, but Priya and Sloan weren't due in until closer to dinnertime, which was still eons away. The girls had all requested to be in one another's bunk, which meant that with four of them still missing in action, the room felt cavernous and—she had to face it—slightly depressing. Chelsea's ruffly bedspread wasn't doing much to perk up the no-frills waterproof canvas of the tent walls.

Finally, when she could bear it no longer, Brynn burst up from her bunk, her shock of short hair bouncing on her shoulders. She smiled at her counselor, Jocelyn "call me Josie," and nodded her head toward the doorway. "I think my friends should be here any minute," she explained. "I'm going to go meet them. Is that okay?"

Josie nodded. "Today is just for settling in. We don't have anything scheduled until dinner tonight, so you're good."

"Awesome," Brynn said. She turned to Chelsea, who was arranging her shoes in a neat row underneath her bed. "Do you want to come meet Jenna and Natalie with me?"

Chelsea looked puzzled. "Why would I do that?"

Brynn shook her head. No matter what, Chelsea would always be Chelsea. Back at Lakeview, she'd been pretty prickly, but as the girls got to know her, they realized that her stoniness was actually just a whole defense thing; her father had been really sick, and Chelsea was trying to be strong by cutting herself off from everyone else. Now that they'd gotten closer to her, they'd started to see a softer side of Chelsea. (And, thank goodness, her father was doing much better these days, too.)

But that didn't mean that she didn't still have her moments.

Brynn smiled. "Never mind. Don't worry about it. I'll just tell them you're waiting for them back at the tent."

She waved good-bye, dashed out of the tent, and hopped off the low wooden porch and onto the ground, kicking up a small cloud of dust in the process. She couldn't believe it! Natalie and Jenna were going to be here *any minute*!

Another summer at camp—albeit a new camp—had officially begun!

▲ ▲ ▲

"Omigosh—you're *here!*"

Natalie winced and glanced up to see perky Brynn practically bounding down the hill toward where she and Jenna had just disembarked the bus. Camp Walla Walla may have been new territory, but Brynn was still Brynn. Screech and all.

Nat smiled. She wouldn't have had it any other way. "We made it," she said, stretching her slender arms overhead and trying to shake some of the bus funk off her skin. "Barely. We finished our last Vanessa Hudgens or Ashley Tisdale quiz about fifty miles back and I almost *died* of boredom."

"Luckily she had me to revive her." Jenna slung an amiable arm around her friend. "Only instead of CPR, I force-fed her gummy bears until her tongue turned rainbow-colored."

"Tell me about it," Brynn replied. "Believe me, you guys don't know boredom. I've been, like, watching Chelsea make her bed up for at least the last seventeen years or so. She brought a *lot* of little pillows." Her eyes went round and solemn. "*A lot.*"

Natalie giggled. "Good. Maybe she'll share. Do you want to show us the bunk, then? Um—I mean the *tent*." As she spoke the word, Natalie felt her heart do a little backflip into her stomach. Jenna had warned the girls via e-mail that in addition to a sportier daily regiment, Walla Walla boasted tents rather than bunks. Natalie's inner jury was still out on the subject of tents. They sure weren't in Kansas—

make that Lakeview—anymore. Good thing they'd all requested to be in a tent together. Strength in numbers and all that.

Brynn's look turned slightly more serious. *Yikes.* Natalie knew that meant the tents were probably . . . tenty. Egad. But after a moment, Brynn rallied, forcing a bright smile on her face. "Yup, and I'm going to give you the grand tour, too! I scoped this whole place out already," Brynn said proudly.

"You really *have* been here for a while, huh?" Jenna asked dryly. Brynn just rolled her eyes.

"Oh—but . . ." Brynn's eyes flickered briefly over Natalie's three oversized bags. "Are those . . . *all* yours?"

"Um, yeah," Nat said, suddenly suspicious. "Why?" She put her hands on her hips. "At least I didn't bring pillows. You said Chelsea brought pillows." Her cheeks were turning as pink as her trunks.

"Oh, uh . . . it's just that . . . well, we're responsible for getting our stuff to the tent," Brynn explained. "By ourselves," she added.

Natalie felt her features cloud over.

By ourselves, she thought. *To the tent. Of course. Awesome.*

Still, though, the last thing she wanted to do was to complain on her very first day of camp. She'd started her first summer at Lakeview feeling pretty cynical about the whole experience, and had sworn to herself that she'd be positive about Walla Walla, no matter what.

Even if that means hauling three bags that are bigger

than I am to my bunk without any help, she realized.

Well, she reasoned, that was the good thing about coming to camp with her friends. She *wasn't*, in fact, without any help. The silver lining made her smile for a moment.

She looked up at Brynn and Jenna, mustering up some cheer. "That'll teach me to listen to my mother about learning to pack light, huh?" she quipped.

Jenna clapped a reassuring hand on Natalie's shoulder. "Don't worry, Nat," she assured her, "you've got us. Just consider us your own personal pack mules. That's what friends are for."

Nat's smile spread wider across her face. "I was hoping you'd say that."

▲ ▲ ▲

As the girls grunted and groaned their way along toward the Oak tent, Jenna eagerly took in every landmark they passed. True to her word, Brynn was all too happy to provide a running commentary on the landscape that, until they'd managed to unload all of their baggage and head off on a proper tour, would have to suffice.

"So, this is Lower Camp," Brynn said, huffing and puffing a bit as she hitched one of Natalie's bags higher up on her shoulder, "where all of the tents are. Then just past our tent there's a footbridge, and past the bridge is the mess hall."

"And our tent is where?" Natalie asked, her voice small and labored. "Not that I'm complaining.

Just . . . curious." She coughed and gritted her teeth, pulling at her trunk as its wheels caught on a pebble in the dirt path.

"We're the last tent," Brynn said brightly.

Natalie only shook her head, causing Jenna to burst out laughing.

"Sorry, sorry," Jenna insisted, seeing the look of exasperation on her friend's face. "It's just . . . of course we're the last tent."

"You *would* think that was funny," Natalie grumbled. "Especially since you probably only want to know where the soccer field is."

And the tennis courts, and the ropes course, and the basketball court, and the waterfront . . . Jenna thought. Out loud she said simply, "Natalie, you read my mind."

"The waterfront is down the slope from the mess hall," Brynn said. "Down the slope is Walla Walla speak for the bottom of the hill. If you use that expression people will think you're fancy. Or at least an old pro. That's what Josie—our counselor, Josie—told me. She wanted to make sure that we Lakeview girls knew all of the lingo. And then all the sports fields and stuff are up the slope from the waterfront, also known as—"

"—let me guess: Upper Camp?" Natalie chimed in.

"You're getting the hang of it," Brynn said, grinning.

"Yay me." Natalie shifted the weight of her trunk into one hand so that she could swipe at the beads of sweat collecting on her forehead with the other. She took a deep breath and continued forward.

Sensing (and maybe even sharing) her exhaustion, the girls shuffled along in silence for a few moments until finally, blissfully, Brynn stopped in her tracks.

"Ladies and . . . well, ladies," she announced grandly, "may I present to you: the Oak tent!" She broke out into a quick jazz square, fingers twitching.

"Please, you're making me tired just looking at you," Natalie protested. She stepped up the rickety stairs and inside. Jenna and Brynn followed close on her heels.

Stepping forward, Jenna careened into Natalie, who had stopped short once she stepped into the tent.

"Ow," Jenna said, reeling back slightly.

"It's . . . a tent," Natalie murmured to no one in particular.

"It's the Oak tent," Chelsea agreed, looking cheerful enough from amidst a mound of throw pillows on her bunk. "Hi, Nat." To Jenna she said, "Your hair is straight," and after a thoughtful beat, "I like it."

"Thanks, Chelsea," Jenna said. Her eyes darted around the room. "It *is* a tent," she agreed. She thought it was pretty cool, herself. "Oh my gosh, it's all great outdoorsy and stuff."

"Yeah, um, at least there will be lots of fresh air and stuff," Natalie said. Jenna could hear a quiver in her friend's voice. "Which I know for a fact because I can feel it blowing through the canvas walls."

Uh-oh, Nat's about to have a total freak-out, Jenna realized. She thought back to Nat's first day at Lakeview, when she had spotted a spider in the bathroom of their bunk and screamed like she'd seen a ghost.

If Nat had been that spazzy about a harmless little spider in the bathroom, what was she going to do, Jenna wondered, when she discovered that the Oak tent didn't even *have* a bathroom? The girls would use a communal outhouse with sinks and outdoor showers that stood behind the tents. Jenna had a sneaking suspicion that Nat had skimmed over that portion of the website.

Yeah, Jenna could just imagine how that was going to go over.

She decided to put off the inevitable for as long as she could. "Where are we all sleeping?" she asked, surveying the room brightly.

Chelsea stood, leaving a pile of pillows in her wake. "This is my bed," she explained, gesturing to her bottom bunk. "And Natalie, I thought you could be on top, 'cause I know you like the top bunk."

Nat nodded numbly.

"I'm here." Brynn indicated a single bunk to the left of the front door of the tent. "Sorry," she said to Jenna. "It was the only single."

Jenna shrugged. She preferred a bunk bed, anyway. She had her own single back at home. "So can I take this bottom bunk?" She pointed to the bed next to Nat and Chelsea's.

"Yup, we thought you could take that, and then Sloan wants a top bunk, so she could be on top of yours—you can save it for her," Brynn explained, "and then Priya would take the bottom bunk there." She indicated the last set of bunk beds in the room. "That other bunk is Josie's. Our counselor. The C.I.T., Anika, is on top."

Jenna nodded, taking in the room. "So who's going to be on top of Priya?" she wondered aloud.

"No idea," Chelsea said.

As if on cue, the door to the tent swung open and in walked a girl that Jenna had never seen before. Everything about her was long, lean, and straight. She was tall, with tanned, slender limbs and straight blond hair that she wore tucked behind a tortoiseshell headband. Her eyes were green and matched the shade of her polo T-shirt exactly. She regarded the girls coolly.

"I'm Avery," she said.

She didn't ask them their names.

Jenna was thrown by Avery's aloof exterior, but decided the best thing to do was just to be friendly. "Hi," she said, smiling widely. "I'm Jenna. And this is Natalie, and Brynn, and Chelsea." She pointed at each of her friends in succession. "We all came from—"

"Camp Lakeview," Avery said, cutting Jenna off. "I know."

She said it in a tone of voice that suggested to Jenna that Avery knew all sorts of things. "Right. So, um, you're a Walla Walla girl?" Jenna asked, forging forward.

Avery didn't bother to reply to Jenna's question. "It looks like there was some kind of mix-up in the office," she said, quickly walking the perimeter of the room. "I'm the only Walla Walla girl in this tent." She said this accusingly, as though Jenna and her friends had orchestrated the situation themselves, on purpose. "Also," she said, stopping her pacing right in front of Brynn. "You took my bed."

Brynn's face scrunched up in confusion. "*Your* bed? But . . . you weren't here. And there wasn't, like, any luggage on the bed or anything. Josie said it was first-come, first-served." She sounded a little doubtful, but Jenna could tell her friend wasn't going to back down. Brynn was psyched about the single bunk she'd scored, and she wasn't about to give it up without a good reason. And why should she have to?

"It's the bed I take every year, in whatever tent I'm in. I had that bed when I was in the Redwood tent, I had it when I was in the Pine tent, and I had it when I was in the Sequoia tent. So I just assumed . . ." Avery's voice trailed off as her eyes narrowed. "You couldn't know, being . . . *new* and all." She somehow managed to make "new" sound like a scathing insult.

Avery stepped forward now, placing her hands on her hips. "So, which bed is mine?" she asked, her voice low.

Brynn was trying to stay tough, Jenna could tell, but her face had gone a pale white. Jenna decided to help her out. "That top bunk there," she said, jumping in. "Our friend Priya is on the bottom. She's really cool."

"Cool," Avery repeated. Her mouth was stretched into a thin line. She didn't sound like she thought any of this was cool at all.

"But, you know," Brynn jumped in, sounding nervous, "you can always, you know, take my bed. I mean, I don't even like sleeping so near to the door and stuff."

"Is there a problem with the beds, girls?" It was Josie, stepping through the tent door just in time to catch the tail end of the awkward conversation.

Jenna noted that Avery's whole posture changed the moment Josie walked in. Her spine straightened and she flipped her hair off her shoulders like a shampoo commercial model. She didn't lose the scowl, though. That seemed to have been burned onto her face like a permanent tattoo. "Sort of," she said.

Josie's eyes swept across the scene, taking things in. "Why don't we go outside to talk about this?" she suggested gently.

Avery glared at the girls and stomped out of the tent, following Josie.

After she'd gone, the room was silent for a moment.

"Well," Jenna said finally, "she seems really sweet."

At that, Natalie exploded with laughter. Soon enough, Chelsea and Brynn had chimed in. But once the giggles had died down, the girls couldn't help but hear Avery's voice, high-pitched and frantic, waft in from outside.

"It's bad enough that I have to be separated from my friends this summer," she was saying, "but now I don't even get my bed?"

"There's no such thing as 'your bed,'" Josie replied, her voice soft but firm. "You've been here forever; you know it's first-come, first-served."

Avery's voice lowered and Jenna found she couldn't make out any individual words. Obviously Avery and Josie were involved in a heated—but quiet—debate. But whatever Avery was saying, she sure didn't sound happy.

"FINE!" Jenna heard at last. "Just FINE!"

Frankly, it sounded like Avery was anything but fine.

The girls stood for a moment, waiting to see if either Josie or Avery would return to the room. When neither did, they looked at one another nervously.

"Huh," Jenna said finally, regarding her friends. "It looks like we've made our first enemy."

No one said a word. Jenna decided a change of subject was the best course of action. Besides, Natalie had to find out the truth sooner or later, didn't she?

"Hey, Nat," Jenna said, forcing herself to sound more enthusiastic than she actually felt inside, "let's go look at the outhouse!"

"Outhouse?" Natalie asked, her voice low and suspicious. "As in, an outdoor bathroom?"

"Yep! Fun, right?" Jenna dashed out the door before Natalie could reply.

So what if Camp Walla Walla was going to take some getting used to? Jenna was up for the challenge. Sooner or later, her positive attitude would have to rub off on the other girls.

Wouldn't it?

chapter
TWO

"So she freaked?" Priya asked, her eyes widening as she made her way up the slope path alongside Brynn, Jenna, Natalie, and Sloan. The slope was pretty . . . slopey, actually, and a bit more of a challenge than she was used to.

"She *totally* freaked," Natalie confirmed, shaking her head in disapproval. "Like, you would have thought that Brynn had taken her pet or her boyfriend, and not just some skuzzy little bed that she thinks she's automatically entitled to."

"Yuck," Priya said, freaking out a little bit on her own. The last thing the Lakeview girls needed was to get off on the wrong foot with their new bunkmate—especially one who was a Walla Walla veteran.

"Sounds like someone needs her aura cleansed," Sloan offered. Sloan was very New Agey and could usually be counted on to suggest something like a good alignment of the chakras or some positive feng shui.

Natalie had a different idea. "Or she just needs to get over herself."

"You could both be on to something," Priya said, eager to keep the peace. She was still hoping that Jenna and Nat were exaggerating about their new enemy. "In the meantime, J—what's that over the clearing there? Just past the waterfront?"

"Oh, that's the shed where they keep the outdoor expedition equipment," Jenna said, her cheeks flushed with excitement. "Isn't that cool?"

"*Expedition* equipment?" Priya asked in disbelief. "They do realize that this is sleepaway camp, not a mountain climbing adventure, don't they?" She was starting to wonder just what she and her friends had gotten themselves into.

"I know, it's so awesome that they take athletics and survival stuff so seriously here," Jenna said, completely misinterpreting Priya's cautious tone. "Hey—I'll race you guys to the shed!"

The last thing Priya wanted to do after the long bus ride to camp was race anyone, even on foot. "Oh, hey—" she protested weakly.

But it was too late. Jenna was already gone, streaking toward the waterfront like a bolt of lightning.

At this rate, Priya worried that she'd never have the energy to last the summer.

▲ ▲ ▲

The first thing Natalie noticed upon returning from the Brynn-led guided tour was that the single bed that had been Brynn's had, while they were out, been replaced by a bunk. The second thing she noticed was that two girls currently sat perched atop that bunk: Avery, looking stony as ever, and another new face, one with rounded pink cheeks, long, brown hair tied back in a low ponytail, and dark brown eyes. The girls appeared to be playing cards, but stopped when Natalie, Sloan, Jenna, Priya, and Brynn walked in.

A hush fell over the Oak tent. *Awesome*, Natalie thought, feeling pretty self-conscious. Clearly Avery hadn't exactly moved into the acceptance stage of her bunk grief just yet. And who was this new person?

Josie popped up from her bed right on cue, which Nat was starting to recognize as a pattern. "Great," she said, beaming at the girls. "You're back. We can do icebreakers. Get to know one another."

"They all know one another already," Avery said sullenly.

If Josie heard Avery, she chose to ignore her. "Let's all make a circle on the floor," she said, settling herself Indian-style and patting the floor on either side of her to indicate that she expected company.

Somewhat reluctantly, the girls arranged themselves on the floor, Natalie dusting furiously at the ground before setting her jean-shorts-clad butt down. Not that she thought it did much good. The tent was kind of like a giant dust pan.

Which it will probably be my job to sweep tomorrow, she thought glumly, all ideas of thinking positively tossed aside for the foreseeable future.

"This is pointless. We've all met," Avery said again, tossing her curtain of silky blond hair back off her shoulders.

"The Lakeview girls haven't met Joanna," Josie said, indicating Avery's brown-haired friend, "and none of you have had a chance to talk to Anika yet.

"G'day," Anika said, grinning brightly. Her teeth were blindingly white and her hair was streaked with highlights that Natalie could tell were totally natural. She would have been jealous if Anika didn't have such a laid-back, warm vibe about her.

"You're from Australia?" Natalie asked, thinking that Anika's accent was really very cool.

"Close. New Zealand," Anika corrected her. "But I've been all over the US on different outdoor adventure trips. So you don't have to worry. You're in good hands with me."

"Oh . . . great," Natalie said, hoping she sounded less panicked than she was feeling. Between the bleak, understated Oak tent and the scary equipment shed that Brynn had shown them, Natalie was starting to get a not-great feeling about how outdoorsy life was going to be at Camp Walla Walla.

"Well, girls," Josie chimed in, gathering her hair into a messy bun at the nape of her neck as she spoke, "there's been a slight change of plans. As you can see, Joanna, who was going to be in the Elm tent, is with us this summer, instead. So welcome, Joanna."

Joanna smiled and looked mildly embarrassed. "Um, thanks."

"So what we're going to do is, I'm going to pass around a roll of toilet paper. Everyone take as many sheets of paper as you'd like."

Natalie's mouth dropped open in horror.

It was bad enough that the toilets were outside. "Is this, like, a *ration* for the summer or something?" She knew Walla Walla was supposed to be rustic, but seriously. Come on.

Avery laughed nastily, not bothering to hide her smirk. "It's a game," she said snidely.

"It's an icebreaker," Joanna clarified, chuckling much more kindly. Her tone was much friendlier than her friend's, and her chuckling much kinder sounding.

Natalie nodded, and when the roll of toilet paper came her way, she carefully ripped off two squares, waiting to see what would come next. Icebreakers usually involved some type of unexpected twist. She had learned this the hard way in the past.

"Now we're going to go around the circle one at a time, and however many pieces of toilet paper you have, you have to tell us that many things about yourself," Josie explained.

Natalie knew this game. They'd played it her first summer at Lakeview, only with M&M's instead of toilet paper. Which said a lot, she realized. What kind of place thought that *toilet paper* was a reasonable substitute for M&M's?

A crazy kind of place, she decided. A rustic, outdoorsy, adventurous kind of place. The type of place that had bathrooms outside instead of indoors. No wonder Avery was so cranky, if she'd been chocolate-deprived for so many summers in a row now.

"I'm Josie," Josie said, waving one square of toilet paper like a teeny tiny flag, "and I'm from Greenwich,

Connecticut. I was a camper here for three years, and this is my second summer as a counselor here at Walla Walla. I go to college in New Haven, and I am studying English. Lit, I mean. So I won't go around correcting your grammar or anything like that." She patted her neat little pile of paper. "There. That's five things. Not counting my name." She turned to Chelsea, who sat directly to her left. "Why don't you go next?" she suggested.

Chelsea looked bewildered at the wad of toilet paper she'd accidentally grabbed. "I don't know if I have that many things to say," she said, sounding nervous. "But, um, okay. I'm Chelsea, and I used to go to Lakeview. I like computer games and books about horses. Oh, and I like gummy bears, too. My mom usually sends me some in a care package over the summer, so I can share with everyone." With that, she crossed her arms over her chest, making it clear she was not going to offer further information, even though her mountain of toilet tissue towered ominously beside her.

Josie seemed satisfied with this, and nodded to Jenna to move on with the game.

"I'm Jenna, and I love, love, love sports," Jenna said, bubbly as ever. "I was so excited when Dr. Steve told us about this camp, because I know it has a great sports and outdoors program. The thing I'm most excited about is ropes."

Now it was Priya's turn. "My name is Priya, and I'm also from Lakeview. Um, one thing that's different about me is that my BFF is a boy. His name is Jordan, and he also happens to be Brynn's boyfriend."

"*And* he's really cute," Brynn chimed in, giggling.

"Okay, Brynn, since you clearly have something to add, why don't you go next?" Josie suggested.

"Sure!" Brynn squealed, leaning forward. Natalie tried not to wince—squealing was, unfortunately, just Brynn's regular talking voice. "I'm Brynn, and as Priya mentioned, Jordan is my boyfriend. I was also a Lakeview camper, and I miss everyone who couldn't be here soooo much. Also, I'm in the drama club at school, and I'm in the camp play every summer. What play are we doing here this summer?"

"An imaginary one," Avery mumbled under her breath, causing Joanna to snicker.

"We don't do plays here," Anika explained. "We're a little more outdoors and athletics-based. But we have *great* cookouts!"

Natalie couldn't help but notice that Brynn looked slightly green to hear this news.

"Speaking of, if we want to get to the opening night cookout on time, we have to get moving with the game," Josie cut in. "Go on, Brynn."

Brynn nodded and took a deep breath, her face returning to its regular peachy hue. "My favorite color is purple and I have a Basset Hound at home named Pokey. After *The Very Pokey Puppy*. Which I can't believe I just admitted out loud."

"We can't believe it, either," Avery muttered, earning a sharp look from Josie.

"I love puppies," Anika announced, sitting up

taller in her place. "And now it's my turn. I'm Anika and I'm from New Zealand."

"No fair," Natalie protested. "We already knew that."

"Hang on, I've got more," Anika said, eyes twinkling. "Last year I toured the rain forests in Brazil, and also completed a bike tour along the California coast. And . . . some of my friends call me Neeks for short."

Sloan explained that she was from Sedona, and that she was a Libra, which was an air sign. Her birthstone was sapphire and she wore tiny blue studs in each ear that sparkled as she spoke. Natalie pointed out that Sloan could also read tea leaves, if you asked her nicely. Avery didn't seem to care, but Joanna peeked at them curiously upon hearing the information.

Next it was Joanna's turn. "Last year I was in the Sequoia tent—"

"With me," Avery put in, looking smug.

Joanna just nodded, looking down at the floor. "And—oh!—sometimes people call me Joey, but not that often, and not camp people, really, and I'm also from Connecticut, and I love horseback riding."

"*And* you requested to be in a tent with me," Avery added. "Right?"

"Right," Joanna said, fingering the sheets of paper in her hand. "But I, um, ran out of paper. That's why I didn't mention that." She looked guilty, Natalie realized. Avery definitely had some sort of hold on her.

Avery was evil. That much was already obvious. She had to be stopped.

"My turn," Avery said loudly, drawing her knees in to her chest and glancing out across the circle. "My name is Avery and this is my fifth summer at Walla Walla. My whole family has gone to Walla Walla, all the way back to my grandma and grandpa, who met when he was in the Birch tent and she was in the Maple. So I'm a legacy. That means someone whose family has been coming here forever."

We get it, Nat thought impatiently. This girl was really too much.

"Um. I got my sailing certificate last summer, so I'm allowed to navigate on our day trips. And I hold the record on the ropes course for the fastest completion." She folded her arms across her chest with satisfaction.

"Not for long," Jenna sang quietly, prompting Natalie to stifle a giggle. She had an idea that Avery wasn't the type of person who took kindly to being beaten or surpassed in any way.

"So, who hasn't gone yet?" Josie wondered, glancing around the circle. "Just you Natalie, huh?"

"Just me," she said, gladder than ever that she'd been careful not to take too much toilet paper. "So, I'm Natalie, and I'm from New York City."

Suddenly Natalie's mind went blank. She couldn't think of a single interesting thing to share with the rest of the group. It was like someone had zapped her with a memory-erasing ray, leaving only a Natalie-shaped shell in her place.

She blinked, thinking hard.

"I know that you and your friends decided to sign up for Walla Walla kind of at the last minute," Josie said, jumping in. "What were you planning to do before you knew you were coming here?"

It was as good a question as any. Even though the answer made her sort of self-conscious. "Right. That. I was taking theater classes. You know, improv."

"Improv," Josie repeated, looking impressed. "Are you an actress, like Brynn?"

"No," Natalie explained, "my dad—"

She stopped abruptly, the sentence barely formed before she bit it back. Her first summer at Lakeview, she'd been reluctant to tell her bunk-mates that her father was a famous actor. She'd learned that people behaved differently when they found out. Some would fake all nicey-nice, wanting to hang out with her in the hopes that they could meet Tad, or some of his famous friends. Others would be cold, assuming that Natalie was snobby and spoiled before they even got a chance to know her.

As it turned out, her friends at Lakeview totally appreciated her for who she was and didn't act weird at all about the stuff with her father. But that didn't make Natalie any less wary about what she chose to share with new people. And she wasn't quite sure she was ready to come out with the story of Tad Maxwell with these new girls just yet.

A quick glance at her friends around the circle told her that they understood exactly what was running through her mind. Her secret was safe with them and they wouldn't say anything until she gave them the go-ahead.

It was nice to have friends who knew her so well. Especially in a place where the bathrooms were outside and the walls were made of canvas. It was comforting.

She looked back up to find that Josie was still waiting for her to finish.

Oh, right. The game.

"My dad thought improv classes would be good for me because . . . I'm shy!" she said in a fit of inspiration.

From her corner of the circle, Chelsea snorted.

"You hardly seem the shy type, Natalie," Anika pointed out, laughing.

"Well, uh, it worked!" Natalie said brightly, hoping nothing more would be said on the matter. She'd have to play shy for the next few days, or hope that everyone else suffered short-term memory loss or something. "Gee, I'm hungry!" she continued, changing the subject ever-so-smoothly. "What was that you were saying about a cookout tonight?"

▲ ▲ ▲

No matter how outdoorsy and rustic Walla Walla was, Brynn decided—or maybe even *because* they were into fresh air and stuff like that—the camp did know how to put on a fantastic cookout!

When she arrived with her tent at the waterfront, the girls found the shoreline adorned with tiki torches and flowered sheets laid across the sand for picnicking. A buffet table stood off to one side, overflowing with salads, condiments, chips, pretzels, and buns, along with every possible type of baked good a person could possibly wish for.

"Whatever happened to old-fashioned marshmallow roasting?" Brynn asked. "Not that I mind the entire bakery set up over there, but you know—there's a reason it's a classic. And I assumed Walla Walla was a stick-with-the-classics kind of place."

"Believe it or not, I heard that we're roasting marshmallows in *addition* to all of the other goodies they've put out here for us. Can you believe it? I might explode after dinner."

Brynn whirled around to find Jordan grinning at her, a plastic lei dangling from around his neck.

"Hi!" she said, leaning in for a quick hug. "And where did you get that?" She tugged at his lei. "I want one." She did. It was bright and festive, and kind of cheesy in a way that was actually hilarious.

He jerked his head toward the bonfire. "They're giving them out over there. Check it out."

She followed his gaze to see Natalie and Jenna ducking their heads down to receive their own leis alongside David and Reed. The foursome made their way over to Brynn and Priya, giggling and sipping at plastic cups.

"Aloha," Natalie said, shaking her lei in Brynn's direction. "That means hello."

"*And* good-bye, and peace," Reed said, poking her in the hip playfully.

"You're so smart," Natalie said. "How did you get so smart?" It was obvious that she was completely smitten with Reed, and Brynn was happy for her friend that she'd been able to drag her cutie three thousand miles across the country for the summer.

Brynn couldn't help but get caught up in her friends' infectious cheer. The night air was crisp and the smell of hamburgers and hot dogs was making her mouth water. "Enough with the plastic flowers," she said. "I'm starving. Let's get some food."

"Wait one sec," Natalie said. She pointed toward where the kitchen staff was dutifully doling out burgers. "I think we need to give Chelsea a minute before we crash her party."

"Oh my gosh!" Brynn clapped a hand over her mouth. Natalie was right, of course. Chelsea stood just by the hamburgers, fiddling with her hair and looking slightly uncomfortable. She looked like she was trying to make conversation. The sort of conversation that good friends wouldn't just go crashing without thinking.

Conversation with a *boy*.

Her friends backed away, giggling and eager to see where Chelsea's flirtation was headed.

▲ ▲ ▲

It wasn't that Chelsea had never spoken to a boy before. It was more that most of the boys she'd spoken to were either somebody's older brother, teacher, or, like, the boyfriend of one of her friends, like Natalie. Natalie had lots of experience talking with boys. She even knew how to make jokes with them, and tell them anecdotes and other interesting things. Chelsea, on the other hand, was finding herself sort of stumped.

It didn't help that this boy's eyelashes were longer than Bambi's. Or that his smile looked like an ad for a toothpaste commercial.

"You're one of the new girls, right? From Camp Lakeview?"

That much was easy. At least Chelsea knew the answer to that question. She relaxed the teensiest bit and nodded.

"Cool. I'm Connor."

"Chelsea," she said, wincing as her voice squeaked a bit.

"Chelsea," Connor repeated, smiling. "So, uh, how do you like *our* lake view?" He swept his hand in the direction of the waterfront, which Chelsea had to admit actually looked very pretty against the flickering lights of the tiki torches. "Get it? *Lake view?*"

She got it. He was making a joke. It was a funny joke, even if it was a little bit corny. The problem was, she couldn't think of a single jokey thing to say back to him. She stared at him for what felt like eons, panicking inside as the seconds ticked by. He probably thought she hated him. Or worse, that she had some terrible disease that prevented her from speaking in complete sentences. He probably thought she was boring.

No. Not probably. He *definitely* thought she was boring.

"I get it," she said finally, her tone short. It was all she could come up with.

Yup, I'm the boringest person from Boringville. With an extra side of boringness to go.

Connor squinted at her. He opened his mouth to say something, then closed it again.

Great, Chelsea thought. She'd blown it. This was what happened when you tried to talk to boys who weren't a teacher or someone's older brother. She'd have to get Natalie to give her some pointers back at the tent later on. It was probably too late with Connor, but at least she'd have some reference point for next time. Assuming there *was* a next time. Maybe she'd blown it. Maybe she'd never talk to another boy for as long as she lived.

She looked up. Connor was still looking at her. Chelsea suddenly realized that she'd gone a very long time without talking. Oops and double oops.

"Uh, I think I'm going to go find my friends," she said.

She dashed across the sand to the rest of her girlfriends before Connor could reply.

She was in such a rush to end the awkward conversation with Connor that she nearly crashed into Jenna, who was doing an impromptu hula and cracking everyone up.

"Ow," Jenna said, stopping in her place and rubbing at her hip. "What was that for?"

"For standing in my way," Chelsea said, pouting.

"Why'd you run away from the cuteness?" Natalie asked. "Did you catch those eyelashes?"

Chelsea rolled her eyes. She didn't want to admit to her friends that the reason she'd bolted from Connor was because she'd been too tongue-tied to act like a normal human being. "Jeez, Natalie, don't you ever think about anything other than boys?"

Natalie merely grinned. "Nope." She glanced at Reed, who was now off concocting some type of food sculpture at the water's edge with David and Jordan. "Well, just the one boy these days. Even if he is being a little grossly boyish right now."

"Here's something else to think about," Jenna said, leaning in conspiratorially. "Avery at ten o'clock."

Sure enough, the lithe, graceful girl suddenly bore down on them, frown in full effect. She was flanked on either side by nearly identical sidekicks, one of whom was the ever-present Joanna, and one of whom was . . .

"Sarah?" Chelsea cried, her mouth dropping open in shock. "What are you doing here?"

This was the best news ever. Sarah was so much fun—great at sports, but also girly and into gossip and magazines. Chelsea was thrilled with this new development.

"She comes to Walla Walla now. Don't you, Sarah?" Avery said, glaring at the girl who had once shared a bunk with the Lakeview girls. Her look was loaded with meaning.

"We had no idea," Chelsea went on, ignoring

whatever weirdness Avery was sending out. "I mean, if you had, like, told us that you were here, we would have totally signed up so much sooner."

"Seriously," Nat agreed. "This is so awesome. Except . . ." Natalie's expression darkened as though a thought had crossed her mind. "Except, you knew we were here, didn't you? Avery had to have told you the second she realized that we were in her tent. Which means that you *also* knew we were in Avery's bunk. So why didn't you come by to say hi to us today? And to tell us that you were at camp?"

Sarah bit her lip but said nothing. Her light brown hair was pulled back into a ponytail so severe that her eyebrows were raised halfway up her forehead, and she wore a wide plastic headband just like Avery's. In fact, her entire outfit, right down to the pastel-colored polo shirt with the little alligator on the breast was a piece-by-piece copy of Avery's.

Well, they say that imitation is the sincerest form of flattery, Chelsea thought. Though the Sarah she knew from Lakeview wouldn't have wanted to imitate someone like Avery.

Of course, the Sarah that she knew from Lakeview would have rushed right over to their tent the second she heard they were there to say hi and catch up.

That Sarah, the Sarah they all knew from Lakeview, had clearly left the building. Or the camp-grounds. Whatever.

"Why should she have?" Avery asked, her voice thick with fake sweetness. "She has new friends now. Better friends. Given her family and all that, it's really a wonder she wasted any time with you guys at all."

"What do you mean, 'given her family?'" Chelsea asked, baffled. She wasn't sure, but she thought Sarah's father was a lawyer. Which was fine, but didn't seem to have a whole lot to do with who Sarah would or wouldn't hang out with.

"What do you mean, *with you guys?*" Natalie demanded, stepping forward.

"Seriously," Jenna echoed. "At least we don't go crying to the counselor the minute we don't get our way. Unlike some people." She shot Avery a meaningful look.

Sarah's face paled, but she didn't say anything.

Chelsea couldn't believe it. This was *Sarah*, after all, the girl who'd orchestrated some of the best pranks against the boys that Lakeview had ever known. Sarah was awesome. Well, usually she was. Right now she was acting kind of like a zombie. An extremely *unhappy* zombie who wasn't interested in reuniting with her old nonzombie friends.

"What's your deal?" Chelsea blurted before she could stop herself. "Why are you acting this way?" She knew it was the wrong tact to take even before the words left her mouth, but she seriously couldn't stop herself. The whole situation was way too bizarre.

"Manners much?" Avery snapped.

Finally Sarah stepped forward. But instead of giving the Lakeview girls any answers or explanations, she merely placed an arm on Avery's shoulder. "Come on," she said. "It's not worth it."

She turned and led Avery and Joanna off toward the drinks table without another word. She didn't look back.

Chelsea bit her lip and stared at her friends helplessly. "Who was that?" she asked finally. "And what has she done with our friend Sarah?"

No one had an answer.

THREE

Dear Adam,

How's it going holding down the
fort? Do you miss me back home? I bet
you don't. I bet you're just excited to have
the whole bathroom to yourself. I can just
picture the mound of dirty towels piling
up on the floor as we speak.

Ugh. You should clean those, dude.
Seriously. I don't want to come home to
a bathroom crawling with grossness.

But really, I want to hear how
everything is at home. Who are you

partnered with for tennis now that
I'm gone, and exactly how badly have
you been kicking his or her butt?
Details, please!

Camp Walla Walla is
NOTHING like Lakeview, but I
l-o-v-e it, even if some of the other girls'
juries are still out. (Nat in particular.
The girl is big on the comforts of home,
ya know?) The camp is all about
outdoor adventures and even has a
motto: Outdoor CORE. CORE
is an acronym. It stands for Compete,
Organize, Rally, Energize. Four things
that I happen to be great at!

We get up early. Like, sunrise
early, and we all head "up slope" (do
you love how I'm picking up the lingo?

I'm all over it) for calisthenics. Then it's breakfast and chores. The worst is outhouse duty, but the way the chore wheel works, you only end up with it every few days, so it's not too bad. Then we have instructional swim and two sports periods. Then lunch, siesta, free swim, and another sport.

That's sports times three. Which coincidentally also equals Jenna times three! And the sports are serious here, too: archery, ropes, sailing . . . I'm going to come home with a whole bunch of new athletic talents. You're going to be crazy impressed, I promise!

It's not all sweat and struggle, though. We do get to chill out at night. Evening activity is usually something fun and more laid-back. Which keeps my less sporty tentmates happier.

Oh! I almost forgot to tell you the biggest piece of news. Sarah is here at Walla Walla! Sarah Peyton. Do you remember her from Lakeview? She was the crazy prankster who totally got along with everybody. She was awesome.

Not anymore. Now she hangs out with this girl, Avery, who's a Walla Walla legacy and acts like we're personally offending her just by daring to breathe the same air that she does. I don't think she likes the idea of newcomers crashing the little camp bubble that she's built.

It's all extremely weird. And in case

we needed another reason to be completely annoyed by her (which, ps, we didn't), she threw a fit on the first day when Brynn took the bed closest to the door. Apparently that's "her" bed, except, too bad, not this time. Later we found out that she likes to take the bed closest to the door so that she can sneak out at night to meet up with her boyfriend. But here's the kicker—

HER BOYFRIEND ISN'T EVEN AT CAMP THIS SUMMER!

So I have no idea what gives. She was obviously just being nasty for no good reason. Some people are like that. Ugh.

Anyway, can you believe it? So much craziness. I'm sure you're sorry to be missing all of the drama. Don't worry; I'll keep you updated on any major developments.

Write back soon.

xoxo,

J

"Nothing like a bee-yoo-ti-ful day on the lake," Chelsea said in a singsong voice.

Okay, fine. So she was being sarcastic. If it was a choice between sailing or nothing, she'd take the nothing. It didn't matter that it was a beautiful day. Sailing was *hard*. Really, really hard.

Seriously. She would have *way* preferred the nothing—even if "nothing" meant sitting stock-still on her flimsy little bunk bed for twelve hours straight—to this "buoy drill" that Christopher, the sailing instructor, had planned for the girls this morning.

Obviously Christopher specialized in unique forms of torture.

"Welcome to sailing," he said with a smile as the girls settled on the sandy edge of the lake.

Next to Chelsea, Jenna had rubbed her hands together gleefully in anticipation. Chelsea just shook her head. That girl was Outdoor CORE to the core, all right. Chelsea needed to borrow some of her positive attitude. If only it could be bottled up and sold.

Still, though, with Christopher's bright, eager smile and glowing, tanned skin, Chelsea, too, had managed to convince herself that sailing could be relaxed, breezy, and fun—nothing at all like what the basic tenets of Outdoor CORE suggested.

Chelsea had been wrong. *Seriously* wrong. Majorly, painfully wrong.

Instead of a morning spent blissfully bobbing along the water's wake, "buoy racing drills," per Christopher's breathless explanation, involved dividing up into two teams to race sailboats.

Fine, Chelsea decided. *I can do this. Never mind that I've never raced when I wasn't on dry land before.* Camp was all about new experiences and whatever, wasn't it?

"We're going to need two teams," Christopher said, rising and stating the obvious. He fiddled with the whistle around his neck and began counting off.

Chelsea's eyes darted back and forth. Her bunk was sharing the sailing session with Sarah's bunk. Not that Sarah had said hello to any of her old friends or anything like that. Nope. Rather, Sarah, Avery, and Joanna had clustered off to one side of Christopher and immediately disappeared behind cupped hands. Chelsea could only imagine what the three of them were whispering about.

Probably what suckers we Lakeview girls are to have ever thought that Sarah was really our friend, she decided, her mouth going sour at the thought.

". . . and, Sarah, with the ones," Christopher said, finishing his count-off. Chelsea blinked. She was a one. So were Priya, Natalie, and Jenna.

Eek! So that meant that Sarah was going to be on the Lakeview team, racing against her new Walla Walla friends?

Or her real friends, more like.

Awkward.

Jenna darted up and patted Sarah's shoulder enthusiastically. "Let's do it!" she said, obviously doing her best to ignore whatever weirdness still existed with Sarah. Chelsea could see the discomfort on Sarah's face, but to her credit, she slowly but surely joined her former friends at their boat.

"Lakeview girls reunited again," Chelsea muttered, glancing at Sarah. Sarah didn't say anything, though—just concentrated on adjusting their boat's sails.

"Yeah!" Jenna shouted, clearly trying to drum up some team spirit and enthusiasm. "We're gonna kick regatta butt, right?" She leaned forward and placed her arm palm down in front of her, obviously hoping for some kind of all-in group-pep gesture that never came.

"A *regatta* is a relay race," Avery said, casually flipping a long lock of hair off her shoulder. "This is a buoy race. Not even, really. A buoy race *drill*." She wrinkled her nose to demonstrate her total disgust in all things Lakeview related. "But of course, you wouldn't know that, seeing as how you wasted so many summers at that other camp."

Chelsea frowned. Okay, so it was true—she knew nothing about regattas, buoys, or sailing, and to be perfectly honest, she wasn't interested in learning. She would much rather play Marco Polo with her friends in the shallow water than risk getting tossed overboard during a heated lap of the competition.

She hadn't planned on speaking aloud. It wasn't worth it to give Avery more ammunition against the Lakeview girls. But the words bubbled up inside of her to the point where she felt like a volcano; she couldn't keep them down.

"Oh yeah? Well it was good enough for Sarah once upon a time!" she shouted, sneaking a sideways glance at her former friend.

But Sarah only looked away.

What had come over her? How could Sarah pretend that she'd never been bunk buddies with the girls from Lakeview? Heck, she'd *been* a girl from Lakeview. But she sure wasn't one anymore.

If Chelsea had been expecting Sarah to chime in and set the record straight about how she had loved every minute at Lakeview . . . well, she had a whole other thing coming. Sarah still wasn't looking at Chelsea, or even at Avery, for that matter. She was perched on top of their sailboat, checking the knots on their sails with incredible focus. Her cheeks, Chelsea saw, were flushed red.

Avery leveled Chelsea with a steady glare, and then cast her eyes toward Sarah, who was deliberately ignoring the whole unraveling scene. She smirked.

"That was then," she said, tossing an arm around Joanna's shoulder and dragging her closer to their own boat. "This is most definitely now."

Ugh, Chelsea thought. The worst part was, she knew that Avery was right. Sarah—the old Sarah, the *other* Sarah, the one who'd been their friend was gone. Totally and completely gone.

The only question was, why? But no one knew the answer to that.

"Psst." Natalie sat up in her bunk, blinking and waiting for her eyes to adjust to the post-lights-out darkness. "Yoo-hoo. Anybody up?"

"Please. Anika and Josie *just* left for that staff meeting. Is anybody *not* up?" Avery snapped from her own top-bunk position.

"You guys, how much do you want to bet that 'staff meeting' is just code for 'party time for the counselors?'" Chelsea asked, giggling.

"Ohmigosh, *totally*," Nat said, gathering her long, thick hair into a sensible ponytail. "Which is why I think we should have some 'party time' for the Oak tent, too."

"Sounds good. Count me in!" Sloan said as she slowly emerged from under her covers.

"I've got brownies," Jenna said. "Mom sent them up in her most recent care package." She snickered. "Except I told her that at Walla Walla, they should really be called CORE packages." She giggled again. "I crack me up."

Natalie tossed a pillow in her friend's direction. "Silly."

"Fair enough," Jenna said, hugging Natalie's pillow toward her. "But now you don't get any brownies." Ever since Jenna's parents had divorced a few summers ago, they had taken to smothering her with elaborate parcels and gifts while she was away at camp. Not that any of her bunkmates minded.

"Mean," Natalie said. "I'd be totally mad at you if it weren't for the fact that I have a much better plan than a brownie party." She smiled to herself at the thought.

"Better than chocolate?" Priya sounded doubtful. "Unlikely. We'll be the judge of that."

"How about . . ." Natalie paused for effect. Her father wasn't the only one in the family who knew how to milk a dramatic moment for all it was worth. ". . . a *raid?* On the Seneca tent?" The Seneca tent was where Reed, David, Jordan, and Connor were staying.

"I like your thinking, Goode!" Sloan said, clapping her hands together and shrieking a little bit with excitement. She placed a hand over her mouth to keep any stray squeaks from reaching the "staff meeting," wherever it was being held.

"Ugh. *As if.*"

It was Avery, of course, spreading her own special brand of sunshine across the tent. She even added a little gagging sound for flourish.

"Thank you for that, Avery," Natalie said when it seemed as though the choking noises had died down, at least momentarily. "For a moment there it almost felt like the tent was having fun together. What would we do without you?"

"It's just, you guys are new, so you don't know," Avery said, bitterness dripping from every word that came out of her mouth. "Raids are, like, *so* not cool here at Walla Walla. No one does them. And you shouldn't, either."

Well, if Natalie had been interested in a raid before, Avery's "warning" just about completely sealed the deal. If there was one thing Natalie hated, it was someone telling her what she could or couldn't do. Especially if that someone was a pouty sourpuss who'd been miserable and negative since minute one of their meeting.

No way, no how, Natalie thought, mentally planning the girls' stealth route down to the Seneca tent. *She's not going to ruin our fun tonight. I won't let her.*

Out loud she said, "Hmm, Avery. Thanks for warning us. But I think we're going to give it a shot, anyway. I mean, there's a first time for everything, you know?"

She meant it, too. Of course, as for the first time when Avery would chill out and just act like a normal human being with the rest of her Lakeview tentmates, well, who knew when that would be?

Natalie knew better than to expect any miracles any time soon.

"Whatever," Avery said, sounding completely bored by the whole exchange. "Suit yourself."

"Shh!"

Snap.

"Ow!"

"Shh!"

"Sorry!"

"Don't say 'sorry,' just *be quieter*," Natalie stage-whispered, taking her role as Raid Commander extremely seriously. Too bad the pitch-black at Walla Walla was, like, *really* black. This was beyond pitch-black. More like black-hole black. The girls kept stumbling into one another, or over dry twigs that insisted on snapping as loudly as possible.

It wasn't exactly subtle. Thank goodness the counselors were all otherwise occupied. But who knew for how much longer?

Well, this makes it a good thing that Avery decided to stay behind, Natalie thought. Being down a bunkmate or two meant they were at least fractionally less disruptive as they stomped through the backwoods path to the boys' tent.

She stopped at a clearing. "That's it," she whispered, waving one hand up so that the girls behind her would catch her signal and, with any luck, stop in their tracks before there was a six-girl pile-up. The crunch of leaves on the ground told

Natalie that everyone had just about caught up.

"Who has toilet paper?" she asked.

Jenna and Priya each waved a double-ply roll. "The better for tp-ing their rafters, my dear," Jenna said with a goofy little giggle.

Natalie nodded, and then realized that in the moonlight her gestures were probably going unnoticed. "Great," she said out loud—still as quiet as she could be. "Who has the toothpaste?"

Sloan and Chelsea stepped forward. "For drawing mustaches and other decorations on their sleeping faces."

Natalie grinned. "Bless their little hearts. They do sleep like babies. Or, I hope they do. Chelsea, I totally think you should do freckles on Connor's face. His skin is just too perfect."

Even in the dark, Natalie could feel the heat radiate off of Chelsea's face as she flushed. Obviously she agreed with Nat's assessment. "I know, right? It's not fair." Chelsea seemed excited at the prospect of spending non-talking, non-one-on-one time with Connor. Which Natalie could understand.

"Have you got your supplies, Nat?" Brynn asked. "I'm going in on the tp thing, so I'm trusting you to handle the boys' outhouse."

"I won't let you down," Natalie swore solemnly, raising a roll of duct tape over her heart like a patriot. "I am going to duct tape all of the bathroom stalls in place—from the inside, mind you, this babe wasn't born yesterday—to completely and totally ruin all of those little boys' mornings." She smiled to think of the boys squirming and complaining, only to eventually slide under the bathroom stalls tomorrow morning bright and early.

Taping the stall doors together was cruel and unusual. In other words, it was just about perfect.

All of those summers at Lakeview hadn't been for nothing. By now, Natalie was an old pro at the delicate art of raiding. And duct tape.

Sloan, Jenna, Brynn, Chelsea, and Priya lined up in a military-style formation, then saluted teasingly. Natalie put her non-duct-taped index finger to her lips and waved them toward the tent. They nodded in unison and crept forward, moving silently but steadily in the cool night air.

Natalie took a deep breath and made her way into the outhouse. It was exactly like the girls' outhouse, except in reverse, meaning that it opened on the left instead of on the right of the building.

"Building," though, was a generous term; it was basically a stack of plywood nailed together haphazardly. Nat grabbed at the door to keep it from slamming shut behind her.

She then decided to hold her nose for the remainder of her raiding activities. It was a boys' outhouse, after all, and members of the boy species were not exactly known for fantastic hygiene. *Blech*.

She slid underneath the first toilet stall, mentally high-fiving herself for wearing her oldest, holiest sweatshirt, the one from her mother's college sorority days that was so threadbare its lettering was mostly just a ghostly outline of silkscreen. Once inside, she

glanced briefly at the rusted toilet seat, shuddered—
ugh, boys—and turned her attention back to the door.
She set about taping up the edge of the door and
then reinforcing her tape. After three layers, she was
satisfied. She pulled lightly at the door. It jiggled in
its frame, but didn't come loose. Perfect for when the
guys came tearing in first thing in the morning.

She dropped to her knees again and slid out
from the stall and into the one adjacent, repeating
the same actions two more times until the next two
stalls had been summarily sealed shut. She peeked
at her watch, noting with some concern that fifteen
minutes had passed. She needed to be getting back to
the rest of the girls outside.

One more stall . . .

She shimmied underneath and sideways,
feeling like a sand crab—

—and then opened her mouth to shriek.

In a flash, a strong hand was over her mouth.
Startled beyond belief, she straightened to standing
and reeled backward against a very strong figure.

"Don't scream or we'll both be in big trouble
for going against lights-out."

It was a boy's voice. A Reed-boy's voice. Natalie
nodded, and he took his hand off of her mouth.

She turned to face him.

And almost freaked out all over again.

He waved his hand in her direction, jokingly
indicating that he wasn't above helping to keep her
quiet if she was going to have trouble controlling
herself.

Which it looked like she was.

Not that it was her fault or anything. Reed was wearing a *face mask!*

An avocado-green face mask, from which his startled blue eyes poked out, round and wide. His lips looked ultrared against the patchy edges of the thick, pasty substance, too. All in all: creepy.

The effect was unnerving. Now that the urge to yelp had died down, Natalie just wanted to collapse in hysterics. She and Hannah had done plenty of home facials back in NYC, but none of their guy friends ever wanted in on the makeshift spa treatments.

"*What* are you doing?" Natalie asked, placing her own hand over her mouth to stifle the laughter that threatened to bubble up.

Reed sniffed indignantly. "It's a thermal reconditioning night mask for sensitive skin." He looked away. "It's from Paris."

Natalie raised an eyebrow. "Really. And you're hiding out in the bathroom with it on because . . ."

Now it was Reed's turn to arch an eyebrow in Nat's direction. "Are you kidding? The guys in my tent would eat me alive if I came to bed this way."

"Fair enough," Natalie said. "I mean, not super-sensitive, you know? But I guess I don't blame them. A reconditioning night mask isn't exactly very boy-ey or anything."

"Which is why you aren't going to tell anyone that you caught me wearing it, right?" Reed asked, a slight panic creeping into his voice. "Why *did* you catch me wearing it, anyway?" he asked, suddenly suspicious. His eyes lit up from beneath the weight of the mask. "Were you *pranking* us? Oh my gosh, you were! You were *raiding* us! You are *so* busted."

Maybe we are. Or . . . maybe not. Natalie took a moment to assess the situation. A guy in a thermal reconditioning mask wasn't really in a position to make demands, after all. "I'll make you a deal," she said, drumming her fingers thoughtfully against the walls of the stall. "*You* don't mention to anyone that the girls from the Oak tent were out on a raid tonight, and *I* won't mention to anyone just how your oh-so-sensitive skin retains that outdoor-fresh glow."

"The guys are going to freak when they see that the bathroom stalls are taped shut," Reed protested.

"More than they'd freak if they learned about your grooming habits? Come on, Reed, even *I* don't go further than the occasional self-styled manicure at camp." She chuckled. It was funny, she thought, to find a boy who liked primping as much as she did. She could hardly blame Reed for wanting to inject a drop or two of luxury into this hard-CORE rugged summer experience.

Maybe this meant that the two of them really were perfect for each other?

"Okay," Reed said finally. "You keep quiet, I keep quiet. It's a deal."

"Shake on it?" Natalie asked, extending her hand.

Reed shook his head no. "Soothing aloe cuticle

cream," he explained, waggling his fingers at her.

Natalie finally collapsed into a heap of the quietest giggles possible. She just couldn't hold back any longer.

There were worse things than being able to trade beauty secrets with your boyfriend, she decided.

▲ ▲ ▲

Okay, so the raid had *seemed* like all fun and games last night, when Priya had been so busy winding toilet paper over the rafters of the Seneca tent to the sheer oblivion of Jordan and his bunkmates. But it wasn't quite so amusing this morning, now that her eyelids felt like sandpaper and she'd staggered through calisthenics. (Jumping jacks at 6:45 in the morning? Really? Wasn't summer vacation supposed to be . . . well, a *vacation*?)

"Wake up, sleepyhead," Brynn teased her, poking her in the side as they made their way down the winding path to the cavernous mess hall. "I don't want you passing out in your oatmeal or anything like that. The last thing we need is for any unusual behavior to give us away. So far, we escaped scot-free." She frowned. "What does that mean, anyway: scot-free?"

"No idea," Priya grumbled. "Don't know, don't care. And anyway, I'm awake," she insisted. "Even though I'd rather not be. How many hours until lights-out?"

Brynn shook her head, her short hair fanning

out in either direction with the gesture. "Check it out. Jordan looks all zombified, too. Guess we interrupted their beauty sleep when we so awesomely raided their unsuspecting little butts. Some girlfriend I am!"

Priya glanced in the direction where Brynn was pointing. Jordan did look like he was dragging this morning. It almost made her feel guilty, for a minute.

Almost. Then she remembered how ridiculous the Seneca tent had looked with swaths of downy white toilet paper hanging from every available surface. And *then* she just had to laugh again.

"Sit next to me," Priya said to Brynn, settling herself on one of the long benches at the Oak tent's designated mess hall table. The goal was to sit as far away from Avery as possible, but since everyone (except Joanna) had the same goal, speed was key. This morning, Priya's slowed reflexes got the best of her; Brynn flanked her on one side, but Avery and Joanna settled on her left, buffered only by a cheerily clueless Anika.

"What do you think we've got up for brekkie this morning, then?" Anika asked, looking way too excited at the prospect of mess hall food. Priya had already learned to manage her expectations in that department. When it came to camp food, Walla Walla and Lakeview were definitely matched in the Thanks-But-No-Thanks department.

Priya peered at a platter that was being slid underneath her nose by a dubious Brynn. "Something yellow. Eggs, maybe? Yeah, I think it's eggs."

"You 'think' it's eggs," Anika repeated.

"Very reassuring."

"Well, I guess it could be creamed corn. But that's more of a lunch thing." Priya smiled to show that she was kidding—sort of. "It's probably not creamed corn."

"It's eggs, you weirdo. Who eats *corn* for breakfast?"

It was Avery, of course, unable to let an opportunity for a swipe pass. Next to her, Joanna snickered nastily.

"No one, of course," Priya retorted. "And by the way—you should let the Corn Flakes people know. I don't know if they got the memo."

Avery rolled her eyes as though Priya's reply didn't even warrant a response. Which was just as well, Priya decided.

She turned back to her breakfast, which turned out to be eggs. She had managed to clean most of her plate—the whole calisthenics-first-thing-in-the-morning thing was making her ravenous these days—when Dr. Steve strode in, clipboard in hand. He looked more serious than usual, which was kind of like saying that he looked serious, period.

He strode to the middle of the room and lifted the whistle that he wore around his neck to his lips, emitting a short, sharp tweet. The entire mess hall was quickly silenced.

"It has come to my attention that members of a certain tent conducted a raid last night," he said.

A murmur rushed through the crowd, causing Priya to exchange a panicked glance with her tentmates. From across the table, Natalie bit her lip. Luckily, though, Josie and Anika didn't seem to realize what was going on. Or that their own campers were responsible for the raid. That would have been bad. *Really bad.*

"As you all know, raids are strictly prohibited—they are an insurance liability."

Priya didn't know a lot about insurance or liability—those were words that her father used when he was on the phone for work—but she had a sinking feeling that in this particular situation, they could only mean bad news.

"And we rely on our campers to adhere to the Outdoor CORE honor code."

Priya swallowed hard. Did Dr. Steve really expect whomever was behind the raid to come up and volunteer themselves to him? And what's more, were she and her tentmates going to do just that?

She suddenly felt ill. And she had a feeling it wasn't from the eggs.

"So I'm glad to report that we already have the information as to which tent is responsible for this . . . egregious infraction."

Egregious infraction. These were ten-dollar words that Dr. Steve was throwing around. Dr. Steve never used words like that back at Camp Lakeview.

Well, this isn't Lakeview anymore, now is it? Priya wondered how long it would take for that reality to sink in once and for all.

She felt a hand clutch at her wrist. It was Brynn.

"Um, he knows it's us," she whispered through

clenched teeth. *"How* does he know it's us?"

Priya made a face. She honestly had no idea how Dr. Steve found out who was responsible for the raid. "Maybe the boys told him?"

Brynn shook her head. "The boys didn't know who raided them," she pointed out.

"Oh, right. That." Priya was at a loss.

That was, until she happened to glance to her left just in time to catch a knowing look pass between Avery and Joanna. Avery glanced up, caught Priya's eye, and winked at her.

Priya's blood boiled. Would Avery really have sold her tent out?

She didn't have to think about it for too long. The answer was beyond obvious.

Yeah, she would have.

"There is one person who knew that we were going out on a raid last night. One person who really, REALLY doesn't like us."

Brynn caught Priya's drift immediately, but seemed to want to give Avery the benefit of the doubt. "I don't know. I mean, being a snitch is lame."

"Well it's definitely mean, but it's not necessarily totally lame if there's a whole Outdoor CORE honor code to live up to and all," Priya pointed out. "And something tells me that Avery is all about the Walla Walla honor."

"Will the girls from the Oak tent please stay after breakfast to assist the kitchen staff in clearing the tables and washing dishes?" Dr. Steve said, earning a round of hooting and cheering from the extremely chipper punishment-free tables.

Priya's eyes flew open. She watched in anger as Avery stood up, smoothed out her shorts, and wandered in the direction of the restroom. She waited about a half a second before leaping up from the bench and scrambling after her.

"Avery," she called, reaching out to the girl as she rested her hand on the door to the girls' room. "What the heck?"

"What do you mean?" Avery asked, her eyes wide and innocent. "What was I supposed to do? With the honor code and everything, I had to tell." She shrugged. "Sorry," she said, not looking the least bit sorry about it at all.

"Yeah, okay, fine, we get it, you're all honest and stuff," Priya said. "But what about *you* and Joanna? I mean, if our tent is punished, that means that you two are on dish duty, too. Right?"

The corners of Avery's mouth turned up in a perfect little smirk. "Wrong," she said. "Exactly, completely wrong. Dr. Steve said that we're exempt from the punishment because we were exempt from the raid. And actually, we get to sleep in tomorrow during calisthenics as a reward for adhering to the Outdoor CORE code. So, um, yeah—you're wrong." She pulled the door to the bathroom open and stepped one foot inside before turning back to Priya again.

"Enjoy kitchen duty," she said. "Hope the raid was worth it."

All Priya could do was sigh.

chapter

FOUR

You are brave, Brynn thought to herself, gritting her teeth together with every step. *You are strong, you are an athlete. Like a contestant on Survivor. That's right— the wily contestant who wins the whole darn thing.*

Except, hopefully, without having to eat bugs and stuff.

"Brynn! Are you even paying attention to what you're doing, or are you all up in your own head?"

"My own head," she called out, embarrassed that Tucker, the ropes instructor, had caught her daydreaming and called her out.

Even though, she thought, *my own head is way better than this whole crazy obstacle course that we've got going on here. I swear, if I look down even once, I'm going to completely lose it.*

She was suspended what felt like miles above the ground, slowly climbing across a rope ladder that stretched horizontally across two tall trees. Even after more than a week at Camp Walla Walla, she had no idea what kind of trees those were. She didn't care, either. Mainly they were the type of trees that existed for the sole purpose of making her life more difficult.

If there were no trees from which to hang ropes, there would be no ropes course at Camp Walla Walla, and therefore no earthly reason why Brynn should find herself crawling across the sky like Spiderman, pretending she was performing her own stunts while filming the latest rock 'em sock 'em action movie. Enough said. She was *not* a method actress.

"You got it, Brynn!" Jackson, Tucker's C.I.T. and the ropes assistant, shouted. Jackson was cute. When he wasn't shouting at innocent girls and freaking them out.

She seriously wanted to fling her shoe at him from high above, but decided she'd probably need it for the descent. Reaching the opposite tree, she quickly found her footing and scampered down, not allowing herself to look at the height she'd just scaled until she was back on level ground once again.

"You got it!" Jackson repeated, coming over and reaching out a hand to high five.

Brynn simply stared at his hand. "I almost died," she said, wishing she weren't whining but knowing she probably was. It was hard to feel high five-y when your heart was still pounding in your chest and there was still a decent possibility that you were going to hurl.

"Nah," Jackson said, affable. "I would have caught you if you'd fallen."

"Great." Brynn rolled her eyes. "Very reassuring. You had a game plan. So you're telling me people *have* fallen?"

He patted her on the back. "Why don't you

go help yourself to some water from the fountain? Hydration is important, you know."

"I *do* know," Brynn agreed. "I'm learning so much here at Walla Walla."

She couldn't help but notice that he hadn't answered her question about the fall. Oh well. It was probably one of those things she was better off not knowing.

"Jackson, you are *so* smart." It was Avery, sidling up to the C.I.T. with an eager grin on her face. "Did you have to get, like, certified to teach ropes?"

Ick. Avery's flirting was as transparent as an ice cube. Did she really think that she was going to be able to get the attention of a C.I.T.? Brynn made a face to herself, then looked up to see Natalie with a similar expression on her face.

She offered a weak cheer for Natalie as her friend made her own way up the first tree of the ropes course, white-faced and looking every bit as panicked as Brynn had felt when it was her turn. She wandered to the water fountain, pressed the button, and ducked under it, gulping the cool water down greedily.

Well, okay, it was lukewarm water. But still, she was thirsty.

I'm learning so much here at Walla Walla, she thought. *Even things I didn't know I didn't know! And never wanted to know!*

"For instance," she said aloud, "one of the many things I've learned at Walla Walla is how much I love standing on my own two feet. On the ground.

Not dangling in the air like a character out of *The Jungle Book.*"

She didn't care that there was no one around to listen; she wasn't quite done complaining and so she grumbled to herself, wiping the last droplets of water from her chin.

She heard a small snort next to her and turned to find Joanna standing beside her, chuckling to herself. It was pretty rare to see Joanna without Avery around, but even rarer still to hear Joanna laugh at anything other than something that Avery (or Sarah, for that matter), had said. No wonder Brynn had been so confused by the noise.

Joanna looked startled, like she herself thought that there was maybe something wrong with listening in on Brynn's conversation—which, Brynn supposed, would have technically been rude, except for how she was really only talking to herself, anyway—and closed her mouth quickly, looking guilty.

Since Joanna voluntarily talking to a Lakeview girl was about as rare an occurrence as a unicorn sighting, Brynn decided she was going to go with it and see what she might discover. "I can't believe you've been coming back here summer after summer," she offered, peering cautiously at Joanna to see how she responded to the direct address.

Joanna remained quiet, but she did nod—albeit shyly.

"And you haven't broken anything yet?" Brynn asked, nodding toward the ropes course. From her spot between the two trees, Natalie clutched desperately at the rope and shrieked something about broken nails and an acute fear of heights.

Joanna shook her head. "You get better at it the more you do it," she explained. "It really does get to be fun."

"I'll just have to take your word for that," Brynn said. "You're not getting me back up there again. I will have to conquer my fear of heights or train to be an action movie heroine some other way."

"That's right, you're the one who loves drama," Joanna said, blinking. "Sarah also—" she paused, biting her lip.

"Sarah told you I love drama?" Brynn asked. If that was true, then it meant that Sarah was talking about her old friends. Which might mean that she was talking about how they *were* old friends. Like, about how, once upon a time, she actually deigned to speak to them every now and then. Brynn suddenly had more questions than she could ask at once running through her brain.

"No," Joanna said abruptly, shaking her head so that her ponytail whipped back and forth against her cheeks. "I just meant that . . . um, well, you should talk to Sarah. You know, because of her connections and stuff."

Brynn's forehead crinkled up. She had absolutely no clue what Joanna was talking about. "What do you mean, Sarah's connections?"

Joanna opened her mouth as if to say something, but just then, two hands planted themselves over Brynn's eyes from behind. "Guess who?"

"Uh, well, I smell Juicy Couture body wash—and fear—so I'm guessing Natalie?"

"You guessed right," Natalie said happily, her pretty face popping up in front of Brynn's own. "I survived. I'm thinking we deserve medals or badges or something."

"Badges would be cool," Brynn agreed. "If we were still young enough for Girl Scouts. Hey—" she continued— "do you know anything about Sarah and act—" she trailed off when she realized that Joanna had slipped away while she and Natalie were chatting.

"Sarah acting really weird this summer? Yeah, I know all about that," Natalie replied, running some water from the fountain over the flats of her palms and splashing it against her flushed face. "Why?"

Jenna rushed up to them, panting and sweating. "Ready for swim?" she asked. She fanned the air in front of her face. "I'm, like, *dying* of heat. I think being up in those trees gets you closer to the sun and stuff. Remind me to wear extra sunscreen tomorrow."

Natalie and Brynn cracked up. "I think you'd have to get a *lot* closer before you needed stronger SPF," Natalie said, "but yeah, let's head over to swim." She made a face. "I just wish they would let me sit out free swim once in a while and read magazines."

"Magazines are not the way of the Outdoor CORE," Jenna said solemnly. She made a tsk motion with her index finger. Nat and Brynn had to concede the case.

"Ugh, I'm never gonna last four whole weeks," Brynn said as the girls marched off. "I think I need to start my own group—Indoor CORE. Our core values will be all about watching romantic comedies and reading gossip magazines. And nail polish. There will also be nail polish. You guys can be my first two group members."

"Fun!" Natalie said, clapping her hands together and breaking into a skip. "I'll write us a cheer or something. And there could be fun uniforms with velour sweats and printed flip-flops."

As Natalie waxed nostalgic about the wide array of silk-screening choices available for their custom track suits, Brynn let herself get carried off into the fantasy. It wasn't until halfway through swim that Brynn realized she never had found out what Joanna really *had* been talking about, what with the whole Sarah and her "connections" thing. But since it didn't make any more sense than Sarah's random cold shoulder did, she decided to just forget about it. It just seemed like the easiest thing to do.

△ △ △

Sarah could hear Natalie's high-pitched voice across the waterfront.

"Drills, drills, drills. I am so sick of drills! Diving drills, treading drills, floating drills . . . can't we just have a good, old-fashioned, honest-to-goodness *free* swim? Look—my magazine got all wet!"

"Well, that's what you get for bringing it down to the waterfront, Nat," Sloan replied logically. "Key word: *water*. We are at the front of the water. Wetness was always a danger. It's not like you needed a Magic 8 Ball to predict that one."

In response, Nat stuck her tongue out at her friend, making Sarah think of how much fun Natalie used to be when they were all in a bunk together back at Lakeview. She glanced around: Avery and Joanna were off doing who knew what. (Unlike Natalie, Avery *loved* drills and thrived on competition. For all Sarah knew, she was off with the lifeguards right now thinking up some new ones and getting extra CORE credit, if there was such a thing.) Maybe now was the time.

Sarah took a deep breath. Yes, now was the time. It was as good a time as any, after all. Wasn't it?

She tentatively approached Natalie and Sloan where they were settled at Natalie's beach towel, Nat playfully swatting Sloan with her (undeniably wet) magazine. Sloan seemed to take it as all in good fun, though.

The girls were so focused on avoiding the tiny sprays of water that rained from the corners of the magazine that at first they didn't even notice Sarah walking up to them. For a moment Sarah thought about running away, forgetting the whole thing, but she reminded herself that she could hardly blame them for not noticing her when she'd been taking as little note of them as possible ever since day one of Camp Walla Walla.

"Hi," Sarah said softly.

Too softly, though, as neither girl looked up to

see her. So she cleared her throat—in her own ears, the sound was as loud as a car engine revving—and tried again. "Hey."

Finally, Natalie dropped her magazine into the sand glanced at Sarah. *"Hey,"* she said, clearly surprised. "Uh, what's up?"

Now that she was actually talking to Natalie, Sarah found that she really had no idea what to say. Where to begin? How to explain? Things had gotten so weird and messy—she couldn't possibly undo it right now, all by herself. Could she?

"I just . . ." she twirled her hair around her fingers nervously. "I just wanted to say that I'm sorry that you guys got busted. About the raid, you know? That's a bummer."

"Yeah," Sloan said, raising an eyebrow. "What with the kitchen duty and all."

She raised her hands up in front of Sarah's face like a commercial for dish soap. "I'm just lucky I don't care about my nails like *some* people here at camp." She cast a pointed—but good-natured look at Natalie, who just shrugged.

"We would have gotten away with it, too," Natalie chimed in, "if it weren't for your friend. She's so stuck on the honor code and whatever. It's like no one here knows how to have any *fun*."

"That's where you're wrong."

Sarah flinched, recognizing the voice. Avery had suddenly appeared right beside her, Joanna in tow, as usual. Yeah, sure, Avery was her friend. But she had an idea that things were about to go from awkward to worse.

"You think we don't know how to have fun?" Avery asked, her voice low. Sarah recognized that tone of voice. Avery was about to challenge the girls to something. Something she wasn't sure they would want to take Avery up on.

Sarah froze in place. There wasn't anything she could say or do. She was stuck—literally—between her two groups of friends.

That was, if the Lakeview girls even still counted as friends. She wasn't sure about that.

"No, I'm sure you're a ton of fun," Natalie said, sounding bored. "What with your snitching and gossiping and all-around grouchiness. Good times."

"Maybe there was a reason that I didn't join you on the raid," Avery said. "Maybe I wanted to see if you'd really go through with it."

"And ratting us out to Dr. Steve and making sure that we got in trouble was just, like, icing on the cake?"

At that, Avery could only smirk. "Look, you guys won. You proved yourselves."

"Awesome, that's what we were going for."

Sarah sighed. She knew Nat well enough to know that the girl didn't care at all about impressing Avery. Sarah sometimes wished she could be as fearless as Natalie, but the point was that Avery was the kind of girl that most people at least *tried* to impress. She just was. Natalie was going to have to learn that, sooner or later.

And it was starting to look like sooner was more likely.

Avery straightened her spine and stepped closer to Natalie, who rose from her towel and flipped her sunglasses off her face and onto her forehead. Sarah thought they looked like rival superheroes from a movie. She almost didn't want to watch. But she couldn't look away, either.

"Great. So I guess that means that you guys are cool with meeting my friends and me out by the lookout point after lights-out tonight."

Natalie looked incredulous. "Why would we do that? So you can get us put back on dish duty? Or maybe something even better this time—maybe we'll be forced to scrub out the outhouses. No, thanks." She turned back to her soggy magazine.

"I'm not going to turn you guys in," Avery said, her eyes flashing. "Duh. I'm going to meet you out there. Why would I turn myself in?"

Natalie put her hands on her hips. She didn't look at all convinced.

"Trust me, you'll want to meet us—" she gestured at Joanna, who seemed a lot less confident than Avery sounded—"if you know what's good for you."

"Now, that just sounds like a threat," Natalie said lightly. "Don't you think, Sloan?"

"Why yes, I do think," Sloan said agreeably. "Not nice, Avery." She wasn't intimidated by Avery, either. Sarah wished she could be as strong and outspoken as those girls were.

"Sarah, tell your old friends what they're missing if they don't come out to the lookout point tonight," Avery said, surprising Sarah with a hard tap on the shoulder. "Now."

Sarah panicked. Here she was, caught in the middle again, just like she had been on that first night, out by the cookout. "You should come," she said, the words barely forming in the back of her throat. "Seriously." She knew what Avery had in mind, and she didn't like it one bit—but she couldn't go against Avery.

Nope. No way.

"Tell her we like to have fun," Avery prompted. "We have, like, a whole game planned for everyone. All of the tents in our age group are going to play."

"And they're all coming out to the lookout point tonight? 'Cause that won't be obvious or anything," Natalie said, skeptical.

"The boys have a different meeting place," Avery said. "But seriously. You have to come. We've got a plan and you're going to love it."

"This is lame. We're not into all of this top secret drama," Natalie said, linking an arm through Sloan's and preparing to head back to the tent to change.

"Wait!" Sarah said, her voice suddenly sounding louder and much more echoey than she expected. Natalie and Sloan both turned, startled.

"It . . . really is a cool game," Sarah said, willing her voice to be even and smooth, like Avery's. She flicked a lock of hair off her shoulder just like Avery did, then remembered that her hair was actually still in a ponytail. *Oops.*

Oh well. How did that expression go? *Fake it until you make it.* It didn't matter if she wasn't as outgoing or as confident as Avery—as long as she pretended that she was.

She could do that.

"You guys should come out to the lookout point for all of the details," she said, her voice ringing stronger with each word. "For real."

Natalie held her hands up in mock surrender. "Okay, whatever. Fine, we'll be there. But if we get in trouble again, you girls are going down with us. Sheesh." She and Sloan exchanged a glance and strode off.

As Sarah watched the girls walk away, she felt a firm hand on her shoulder. "Good girl," Avery said, her eyes twinkling. "They *will* love our game, you know. It's totally *killer*."

Sarah managed a weak smile. "I know," she said. "I know."

She only wished she could be as sure as Avery sounded.

chapter FIVE

Breathe, Sloan told herself, willing herself to be calm. Big, cleansing breaths. In, and out.

"Have you noticed how the *dark* here is, like, really, really dark?" Brynn asked, her voice a hoarse whisper.

The girls slowly made their way upslope along an overgrown back path, careful to be as stealthy and silent as they possibly could. Just because they were going along with Avery's plan didn't mean that they had to be dumb about it. No sense getting caught a second time. Dish duty once was way bad enough.

"That's the thing about dark," Chelsea said dryly. "The darkness."

"I think I saw a snake!" Natalie chimed in, sounding deeply freaked out.

Okay, Sloan thought. *They're going to lose it. Not cool. We'll definitely get caught if we fall apart right now.*

She stepped to the front of their little cluster. "Natalie, you didn't see a snake." She had to get her friend to calm down.

"But—"

"You didn't," she repeated with as much authority as she could muster. "It's not even a possibility. We don't go there. And yeah, Brynn, it's totally dark out here. So what we're gonna do is focus on our breathing."

"*That's* your big solution? Air?" Chelsea snorted, incredulous.

"I know, it doesn't sound like much. But still, trust me, it'll totally calm you down. Pick a color and a temperature for your breath. Like, mine will be cool blue."

"That sounds like a toothpaste," Chelsea put in.

Sloan decided to ignore her. "Mine will be cool blue. When I breathe in, I can see it traveling to all of the corners of my body, filling up the spaces in my fingertips and underneath my toenails and all of that stuff. And when I breathe out, it takes all of the ickiness—including the fact that I am majorly creeped out being out here alone with you guys in the dead of night—with it." She demonstrated for them, inhaling deeply so that they could hear and letting her chest puff out slightly, then exhaling for effect, hunching her shoulders and slumping over as the air rushed out of her body.

"See? All calm. Yay."

Chelsea was still grumbling her skepticism, but around her Sloan could hear her friends taking gulping breaths in and blowing out with all of their force. Okay, so maybe they needed some practice with the meditative breathing, but it was better than all of the freaking out and imaginary snakes and ghosts and other grossness. *Much* better.

"Good, good," Sloan said, starting up the procession again to get the girls to the big rock. They crept along for a few beats, the crackle of leaves under their feet and the big, deliberate breathing (that even Sloan had to admit sounded sort of silly, even if it was kind of working for them all) the only sound in the chilly night air.

After a bit, they heard soft voices.

"We must be close to the clearing," Sloan said. They quickened their pace, and were soon rewarded by the sight of a cluster of girls milling around, yes, a big rock.

"This must be it," Sloan said, crashing forward and looking for Avery. She found her leaning against the rock, flanked on either side by the ever-present Joanna and Sarah. The rest of Sarah's tent—and, as promised, the rest of the girls from their age division—were gathered there as well, casting shadows against the rock in the moonlight.

"You made it," Avery said, gathering her long hair into a quick ponytail and stepping toward them. "Good. You're the last ones. Now we can get started."

"You still haven't told us what your super-exciting and fantastic game is," Sloan pointed out. "Clue us in, pretty please?"

"It's called Assassin," Avery said, drawing out each syllable of the word.

Immediately the rest of the girls, the Walla Walla lifers, began to buzz.

"Still no idea," Sloan said simply.

"I know," Avery said. "How sad. It's simple enough: Everyone gets a spoon."

"That *does* sound simple," Sloan quipped. "And boring." Who wanted a spoon without ice cream or other yumminess attached to it? No one, that was who.

"Everyone gets a spoon," Avery continued, ignoring the jab, "and everyone gets a name. Don't tell anyone whose name you draw. That person is your target. Your job is to 'kill' your target."

"That sounds like a major violation of the honor code," Priya said, sounding doubtful.

"It's a *game*, duh," Avery said. Even in the dark, Sloan could see her rolling her eyes. "You don't do anything to them. You just have to take their spoon. Once you have their spoon, you inherit their target. In the meantime, you avoid having your own spoon stolen. The last one standing wins."

"Is there a prize?" Jenna asked, her eyes shining. Sloan was still seriously wary of anything Avery had cooked up, but of course Jenna was all over the game. Jenna *lived* for games.

"Bragging rights," Avery said simply. "Maybe some ice cream from the canteen."

"There should be ice cream," Jenna asserted. "Ice cream is a good prize."

And it made sense with the spoon, Sloan thought. She liked the idea of putting the spoon to practical use.

"Okay," Avery said, waving her hand impatiently. "Ice cream, whatever. So, ok, rules: We'll all pick names tonight. Then tomorrow at breakfast, grab yourself a spoon. You're allowed to hide your spoon, but not on your body or anything. So no stuffing it down your pants and stuff."

A few of the girls giggled at that.

"And you can totally do whatever it takes to get your target's spoon."

"What, like go through their stuff and whatever, and try to figure out where they're hiding it?" Natalie asked.

"Go through their stuff, spy on them, listen in on their conversations, anything you need to do," Avery confirmed. "That's what makes it so much fun. You learn a *lot* about your fellow campers."

Sloan thought it was pretty funny that Avery didn't express the slightest interest in getting to know the girls from Lakeview in conversation, but seemed totally content to go through their stuff and uncover all of their innermost secrets. It didn't seem like the most direct way to get to know someone.

"You learn a lot, huh?" Sloan mused.

Was it Sloan's imagination, or did Sarah's face pale at that comment? It was hard to tell in the moonlight, but Sarah was definitely starting to look a little queasy.

"So you can take someone's spoon whenever, wherever?" Jenna asked, still hung up on the rules.

"Almost, but not quite," Avery replied. "The mess hall is off-limits. When you're in there, the game is on hold. You need one place where you can let your guard down. Otherwise people get way too wired up. You'll see, there's like a whole 'Assassin-mood' that comes over the camp. So, yeah—safe zone. But beyond that, there really are no rules."

"Cool!" Jenna said, clearly eager to get started.

For her part, Sloan didn't care quite so much. She wasn't competitive the way Jenna was, and she didn't love the idea of her fellow campers snooping through her stuff and eavesdropping and all of that. Then again, snooping was kind of fun when you were on the snooper side of things rather than the snoopee.

So maybe it was worth a shot.

She shrugged. "Okay, I'm in."

"Great," Avery said, grinning a small but contented smile. She held out a baseball cap filled with what Sloan realized were tiny, folded-up slips of paper. "Pick a name."

Sloan closed her eyes and stuck her hand in the hat, letting her fingers close around a piece of paper. She fished her paper out, unfolded it, and quickly read the name on it. She looked at Avery and nodded, then slipped the paper into the back pocket of her cutoff shorts.

"Next," Avery said primly.

Jenna practically lunged forward, her hair bouncing every which way. She pulled out her own slip of paper, read it, and pocketed it.

One by one each of the girls moved toward the hat, and one by one each received her assignment. As papers were balled into tiny wads and slipped into shoes, socks, pockets—some even tucked under headbands—the mood in the air shifted. It was a small but noticeable change, Sloan realized. Something about the glint in people's eyes, or the wariness with which they all now regarded one another. Everyone was sizing everyone else up. Everyone was suspicious. No one knew who had them as a target, and no one wanted to give away who they had.

If Sloan had thought that things were tense at camp between the Lakeview girls and the Walla Walla girls before, she was in for a whole new thing now. That was *nothing* compared to the cloud of distrust that hung in the air right now. That, back then, had been love and friendship and puppies and rainbows.

But now? Now things were about to get interesting. *Way* interesting.

And all at once, Sloan kind of couldn't wait.

The game was *on*.

Dear Daniella,

Greetings from Camp Walla Walla! Bet you never thought I'd last this long up here, given the whole Outdoor CORE thing and all of that. I may not be a girly-girl like Natalie, that girl I've been telling you about, but I'm not exactly the rugged type. Oh, well—maybe all of this toughening up will prepare me for the next monster winter outside Beantown?

Meanwhile, Outdoor CORE aside, apparently there's a whole other tradition here that the campers play (behind the staff's back, natch)—a game called Assassin. Have you heard of it? I never had before I got here, but Avery swears it's HUGE in Greenwich, CT (where she's from).

Of course, according to Avery, everything she likes is, in reality, HUGE some place that's other than here. One thing that's definitely kind of

huge? Avery's ego. Blech. She is such
a pain.

But anyway, Assassin: It's
actually pretty cool. We're each assigned
a secret "target" and have to steal our
target's spoon. (Did I mention the
spoons? Yeah, there are spoons.) Once
you capture someone, you inherit their
target. And then the last one in the game
wins . . . something. It's a little unclear.
There might be ice cream, I don't know.
That would at least explain the spoons.
Or maybe you just win an Avery-sized
ego-bump. Who knows? Whatever,
everyone's playing, and even though Avery
is kind of annoying, it's fun.

And the interesting, maybe-kinda
best part of it all? My target is this guy

named Connor. He's pretty cute. We talked at the cookout on the first night, and ever since then we've sort of smiled at each other on our way to and from the mess hall and stuff. Natalie and Jenna think he likes me. I mean, they're probably just exaggerating, or getting carried away, but still, it could be cool if he did. Or not. We'll see.

Did I mention that he's pretty cute? To confirm: there is cuteness.

But, okay, whatever. No big deal.

Not much else to report. I took my lifesaving test the other day and passed. So the whole Walla Walla boot camp mentality is good for some things, at least. And Sarah—Sarah Peyton? From Lakeview? She's still being a weirdo and pretending we were never all friends. I think a tad bit of Avery has rubbed off on her. Double-blech.

Anyway, write soon and tell me what's been going on up in Boston. How's that summer school program in Beacon Hill? And have I mentioned you're crazy for voluntarily choosing extra school for your summer vacation? Extra school! It defeats the whole purpose of vacation!

And on that note, I've gotta run. I've been getting the hairy eyeball from some of the girls in the bunk while I write, and it's starting to weird me out. Everyone's been so paranoid since we started this game! The demand for ice cream is higher than I thought.

Miss you,
Chelsea

"Did I ever tell you that I'm allergic to nature?" Natalie sneezed for emphasis, turning away from Reed as she did so and covering her face with her hands. She came up for air still sniffling delicately. "See?"

"I think they have pills for that now," Reed replied. "You can buy them at most major drugstores."

"*So* not the point," Natalie said. "I'm just saying: I prefer to enjoy the great outdoors from the comfort of indoors. There's nothing wrong with that. Sue me. Or call me crazy. Do whatever you want to me—as long as that doesn't involve dragging me on a 'division-wide nature walk.' *Achoo.*" She sneezed again for good measure.

"You are preaching to the choir, Nat," Reed assured her, stumbling slightly over a rock in their path. "Identifying leaves all morning is hardly my idea of a good time. *Ow.*" He stubbed his toe on a tree root he hadn't seen protruding from the earth and lurched forward, grabbing on to Nat's arm as he did so.

Natalie smiled and grabbed him right back, steadying him. Okay, so maybe every now and then nature managed to get it right. "Whoa, Nellie," she said.

"Nature is against me," Reed said. "Nature hates me."

"I think you hurt nature's feelings," Natalie pointed out. "The leaves are just having a little bit of harmless payback."

"Harmless?" Reed paused on the path and lowered himself until he was sitting on a relatively flat rock, dusting it off as best as he could before he settled in. "What if I get blisters? It's not like I can just run off and get a pedicure here in the middle of the wilderness. My feet are going to be *rough* when I get back to L.A."

"Uh, yeah, that's a bummer," Nat mumbled, a little bit thrown. She wasn't used to crushing on a boy who was more worried about his nails than she was about her own. Then again, she'd been dreaming of the paraffin treatment offered at the little day spa around the corner from her New York apartment basically since they left the tents that morning. So she couldn't exactly blame him for craving a little luxury as much as she was. Maybe it was like she had thought the other night at the raid, after finding him with the face mask on.

Maybe they were just completely and totally perfect for each other.

"Hello, fellow slowpokes," it was Brynn, huffing and puffing her way down the path with ruddy cheeks and a look of frustration. "We're losing the rest of the group. What if we get separated and lose our way in the wilderness and have to live off of weeds and drink mud and all that to survive?" She flung her hand toward her forehead and swooned dramatically.

"I think we're, like, ten feet from the clearing at the big rock, Brynn," Nat said dryly. Not that she'd expect any less overblown a performance from her friend.

"Right. Cool. Sure," Brynn said, surveying the scene and nodding to herself. "Good news about the mud. But what are you doing on the ground?" she asked, finally noticing Reed hunched over his sad, sore feet, rubbing them mournfully.

"Blisters," Natalie explained. "He needs a salt bath or something."

"I think we're supposed to do a lake swim right after this. The water should help," Brynn said. She strode forward and pushed past Natalie, holding out her hands to Reed. "Up. We've got to get back to the group. You can be my nature walk buddy," she said, her eyes bright and her smile perky. Almost as an afterthought, she turned to Natalie. "I mean, we can *all* be buddies. All three of us."

"Um, yeah, sure," Natalie said, wondering if she was the one going crazy, or if it was everybody else. Was Brynn *flirting* with Reed? With the whole helping him up, and asking him to be a buddy, and the big, bright smile?

No. No way. Brynn would never do that. First of all, Brynn had a boyfriend. And B, she *knew* that Reed and Natalie were together, that they had come to camp together. They even had a history together! They went way back, to L.A. and the Oscars. Obviously Natalie was just losing her mind and reading things wrong. Just like thinking that Reed was being a little bit whiny for not being able to hack the nature walk when, in truth, she *completely* agreed with him. Heck, she'd been whining since the whole thing started.

And actually? She wasn't about to stop now.

She glanced up to see that the whole time that she'd been lost in her own thoughts, Brynn and Reed had managed to make their way more than a few paces ahead of her. *Whoopsie.*

"You guys," she called, scampering after them, for once not giving even the slightest consideration to what the running must be doing to her pedicure, "wait for me!"

chapter
SIX

Sarah was famished.

Okay, so this wasn't exactly her first summer at Walla Walla, but somehow her body never got used to how demanding all of the outdoor activities at this place were. It always came as a huge surprise when she made her way to the mess hall and realized, with a disbelieving start, that her stomach was growling loudly enough for her parents to hear her back home.

Too bad there was only *camp food* to quiet it.

Maybe that's why they run us so ragged here, she mused. *So that we're too tired and hungry to complain about how awful the food is.*

It was a theory.

She felt an elbow in her ribs and turned to see her tentmate, Hailey, a tall stringbean of a girl with glossy black hair and an explosion of freckles, looking impatient. "I know whatever is waiting for us in there is probably not worth getting all pushy about, but can you . . . push a little?" She meant through the throngs of waiting campers. "I'm gonna pass out if I don't get something to eat ASAP."

"Me too," Sarah agreed. "But keep in mind that it might be 'sloppy joe surprise' today." *As if any normal person would be interested in a surprise like that.*

"Surprise!" Hailey said, waving her fingers like a jazz dancer. She spread her hands out and waggled all of her fingers. "It's totally inedible." The two girls laughed, and Hailey linked an arm through Sarah's. "I don't even care. I'm going to eat whatever they put out. Including the cutlery."

"Good thing you've got an extra spoon stashed back in the bunk," Sarah said as the doors to the mess hall opened and the campers began to trickle in.

She was referring to the fact that this morning, just before the nature walk, Hailey had "killed" her target: Jordan. She'd found his spoon in—*ugh*—his laundry bag.

Sarah shuddered. "But you can't eat with that thing until it's been boiled, sanitized, disinfected, and then boiled again. It was in his *laundry*. Like, hanging out with his dirty socks and stuff."

Hailey giggled as the girls found seats at their table and waited for their counselor, Tara, to get their food. "I wasn't planning on *eating* with it. It's more of a trophy. And anyway, that's the whole point of Assassin," she reminded Sarah. "You get to just be a big, fat spy, and no one can give you any trouble about it. You can root through people's dirty laundry."

Sarah shook her head. "I don't think you're supposed to take that expression literally, Hals." She poured herself a glass of bug juice and gulped it down eagerly. "Besides, did you learn anything all that interesting about Jordan in the process, anyway? Any embarrassing love letters from Brynn?"

"No such luck. Only that his mom wrote his name on the inside collar of all of his T-shirts," Hailey admitted. "Which is kind of boring. But a little cute. I love the idea of his mom putting labels in his shirts and helping him pack up his trunk."

"Extremely cute," Sarah agreed.

As she reached for Hailey's glass to pour some juice for her friend, Avery swung by their table. Even though they'd just spent over an hour traipsing through the woods, sweating and dodging low branches and stuff, Avery didn't have a hair out of place. Frankly, Sarah doubted if Avery had ever had a bad hair day in her life. It really wasn't fair at all.

"Hey girls, how's it going?" she asked, grinning and leaning in toward her friends. "Good work with Jordan, Hailey. Someone had to kick the game off right."

"Jordan has his name written in all of his T-shirts," Sarah offered, wishing she had a better scoop for Avery. Avery generally liked a good scoop. A boy with name labels in his clothes was not gossip.

"*That's* the best you can do?" Avery widened her eyes and her smile at both of the girls. "Please. This game is *rife* for digging up dirt. I, for one, cannot wait to get the deets on all of the Lakeview girls." She let her eyes wander to the table where the Oak tent ate, surveying them all hungrily.

Was it Sarah's imagination, or did Avery's eyes

linger on Natalie for just a beat longer than on the others? And if so, what did that mean?

Was Natalie Avery's target?

Sarah suddenly felt her insides run cold.

If Natalie was Avery's target, then Avery would be practically stalking Natalie until she captured the girl's spoon. This meant that she'd be combing through the Oak tent with every ounce of energy that she had.

And Avery could be *extremely* energetic when she wanted to be.

This was a disaster.

The last thing that Sarah needed was for Avery to go through all of Natalie's stuff and find out . . .

Well, and *find out*. Find out all of the things that Sarah hadn't told her.

No. No way. That wasn't going to work. And what was more, Sarah wasn't going to let it happen. She was going to have to watch Avery extra carefully going forward, to stick to her like glue and monitor all of Avery's attempts to uncover Natalie's— and therefore, Sarah's—secrets.

This meant that she was going to be mighty busy.

Sarah was still deep in thought, assessing the possibility of damage control and wondering just how crazy she might wind up looking—to Avery or to any of her other friends, for that matter—when Tara deposited a steaming platter of what appeared to be overcooked spaghetti with watery marinara sauce on the table in front of her. She barely blinked when Hailey reached past her for the serving tongs.

"Wait—did you want some?" Hailey asked. "You totally just took a trip to space-out-ville. Helloo, Sarah? Yoo-hoo?" She waved a hand in front of Sarah's face.

"What? Oh—no, thanks," Sarah said, snapping out of her reverie all at once. "You go ahead."

"Good, 'cause like I said, I'm starving, and there's only so much they can do to ruin pasta."

"True," Sarah said with resignation. "But I'll pass, anyway. I think I just lost my appetite."

▲ ▲ ▲

"Thank goodness for cookouts!" Natalie exclaimed as she, Jenna, and the rest of the Oak tent made their way down to the waterfront for an evening bonfire and barbeque. "I thought I was going to starve to death after those sad little noodles we had at lunchtime."

"Lunch was grossness, but I saw you scarfing down some gummy bears during quiet hour," Jenna pointed out.

"Fair enough. But there's always room for barbeque! I think I'm going to have a hamburger *and* a hot dog."

"Go wild, Natalie. You only live once," Jenna deadpanned.

"What, you're not excited about the campfire?" Sloan asked, coming up behind the girls and shimmying her way between them.

"It's not that," Jenna explained. "I'm just worried about all of us being away from our tents for so long. There's way too much potential for some major Assassin recon."

"*Recon*," Nat giggled. She loved how her friend was being all super-commando about the game. "Aye, aye, captain."

"I'm not a *pirate*," Jenna said, shooting Natalie a withering look. "I'm an assassin. You are, too."

Natalie raised an eyebrow.

"It's just . . . okay, so I'm taking the game a little more seriously than some people are," Jenna conceded. "So what's wrong with that?"

"Nothing is wrong with that whatsoever," Natalie said reassuringly. "As long as you don't need me painting my face in camo colors and getting all into it with you and stuff. I'm more of a 'support you from the sidelines' kind of gal. Like, I'll look for my target and hide from whomever has me as a target. But there won't be any recon involved. You can't make me." She folded her arms across her chest in a "so there" gesture.

"Wouldn't dream of it," Jenna replied. "Though I seriously can't believe that you're the same person who organized a raid the other night. All on your very own."

"That was different," Natalie pointed out. "There were boys involved."

At that, Jenna had to laugh. Of course things were different for boy-crazy Natalie when there were boys involved. Meanwhile, Sloan was scouring the beach to see which of their friends had already arrived. "There's Jordan," she said. "I guess he doesn't have to worry about guarding his domain now that he's been killed."

"Good," Natalie said, "because everyone else is being so spazzy that the more people who are bowed out, the better. Have you noticed how Joanna has been walking around with eyes the size of satellite dishes these days?"

"I guess because the whole game was Avery's idea, she'd be totally humiliated if she were one of the first people out of the game. So she's got her guard up." Jenna almost looked sympathetic, Natalie noted. It was hard not to feel at least a little bit bad for Joanna. Being Avery's mini-me couldn't be that much fun.

Then again, it was also hard to be sympathetic to someone whose best friend's life mission was to make you miserable.

Suddenly the girls heard shouting, followed by two boys crashing through the bushes and down to where the firepit had been set up. Natalie recognized them as Neal and Justin, two of Jordan and Reed's tentmates. Neal appeared to be chasing Justin. Over his head, Neal waved a small silver spoon in triumph.

"Why is Justin running away? Once Neal has the spoon it's over, right?" Natalie asked Jenna. "Am I getting the rules wrong? What is all of this . . . running?" Hadn't they all had enough with the stamina and exertion and sweat for the afternoon? Heck—for the whole *summer*? Couldn't a person just toast a marshmallow and call it a day? Summer was supposed to be a time for relaxing, for Pete's sake.

Jenna shook her head. "You're not wrong, but my guess is that Neal is just going for dramatic effect. *Boys.*"

"And the counselors don't care? Even though we got in trouble for sneaking out for a raid?" Natalie seethed at the injustice of it all. She was still bitter about being forced to wash dishes. Dishes were her very least favorite chore.

"We are not Miss Perfect Princess Avery," Jenna said. "Avery couldn't violate the honor code if she tried. Besides, technically, Assassin does go against the honor code, but the thing is that the counselors and the rest of the staff turn a blind eye as long as we're not too obvious about it." At Natalie's questioning look, she said simply, "I've been doing some asking around."

"They're *wrestling*," Natalie said, pointing to where Neal and Justin had practically tied themselves in a knot on the ground. "How is that not obvious?" She could hear the grunting over the din of the rest of the campers, and the boys were kicking up huge clumps of dust and sand as they rolled all over the ground.

"*Boys*," Jenna said again. "If anyone asked, they'd just deny that it had anything to do with Assassin."

"Boys," Sloan echoed. "Ugh."

"Really," Natalie said. "Speaking of . . ." she let her voice trail off and she squinted to see if she could make out Reed among any of the other hyper little y-chromosome types. Nope. He wasn't there yet.

"Looking for your Prince Charming?" Sloan teased.

"Maybe," Natalie said, smiling softly. Okay, so she got a little giddy at the thought of Reed. There were worse things.

"You can't fool me, I'm psychic," Sloan reminded her. "Right now your aura is so pink it's practically a Strawberry Shortcake movie. You're in *lllluuuuuveee*."

Natalie arched an eyebrow. "Like. I'm in like. And it doesn't matter, because if he isn't here yet, then you guys are stuck with me, and I say, enough boy talk—bring on the hot dogs!"

The girls didn't need any more prompting than that. They proceeded to stuff themselves silly with cookout food. Anika and Josie joined them, along with Avery and Joanna (most likely at Josie's suggestion, Nat suspected, but still). For a moment it almost felt to Natalie like the entire bunk was getting along and they'd fallen into a nice Walla Walla groove, Outdoor CORE or no.

The sound of hooting and hollering farther from the shoreline and toward the path down to the waterfront pulled Natalie's attention away from her tentmates and toward Dr. Steve. Ever-present clipboard in hand, he made his way to the head of the beach where the lifeguard shack stood, his eyes sparkling with excitement.

"Are you all having a good time tonight?" he called.

Thunderous cheering greeted him. Natalie's mouth was still full, so she had to settle for kicking her feet against the sand. It wasn't actually noisy, but it was still satisfying, anyway.

"Great," Dr. Steve went on. "Because I've got some news that you're going to love! This Friday will mark the start of our annual Outdoor Adventure Weekend!"

Next to Natalie, Avery put two fingers in her mouth and whistled. The sound pierced Natalie's eardrums. Clearly Avery thought this was very good news indeed.

For her part, Natalie was a tad suspicious. "Outdoor Adventure Weekend" sounded suspiciously like three days of nature walks. Maybe worse.

As if to confirm her worst fears, Dr. Steve raised his hand to quiet the crowd. "Some of you are familiar with Outdoor Adventure Weekend, but for those of you who aren't, just know that it is exactly what it sounds like. It's a camp-wide event, though the divisions go through the different legs of the weekend separately and in slightly separate locations. This is meant to foster teamwork and camaraderie among your peers. Your division will be starting with a day-long hike, followed by a two-day overnight. We'll spend one day fishing and one day boating."

From across the circle where their tent had settled down, Natalie could see Jenna doing a happy dance in her seat. Avery, of course, only smiled more and more widely, until it looked like she was possibly going to swallow her own face whole. Joanna seemed pleased, and Anika no doubt was already anticipating spearing dinner from the river with her own bare hands or something equally pioneerlike.

For her part, Natalie wanted to throw up. And she doubted it was from the three hot dogs she'd eaten. Outdoor Adventure Weekend sounded dirty, tiring, and totally scary. She was really starting to wonder if she was truly cut out for Camp Walla Walla.

I could still get out of it, she thought to herself. *Mom would be annoyed at me for bailing after begging so hard to come to camp, but she'd pull me out if she thought I was miserable. And Dad would just be excited to think that I was going back to acting classes.*

Her stomach hitched uneasily.

It would only take one phone call . . .

She looked up and happened to catch Jenna's eye. Jenna flashed a quick thumbs-up, which Natalie knew was Jenna's way of reassuring Nat that no matter what, they'd get through the weekend together.

Natalie knew that going home wasn't an option. Not when all of her girls were here and counting on her.

Her stomach flipped again. This time, though, it was for a different reason. It wasn't that she was having second thoughts about the weekend—far from it, every thought she had screamed to avoid it at all costs—but rather, that she knew no matter what, her Lakeview girls had her back. She wouldn't be going through this weekend alone.

Yes, she was probably going to suffer, and her

allergies were *definitely* going to take a serious hit, and the soles of her feet were not going to be improved by hiking one bit.

But she'd be suffering alongside her bestest friends.

Which was *kind of* the same thing as fun, wasn't it?

▲ ▲ ▲

One of the best things about an Outdoor Adventure Weekend, Priya decided, was that it kept all of the counselors busy at a late-night staff meeting, leaving the girls of the Oak tent on their own after lights-out.

Well, all of the girls except one.

"Where *is* Chelsea?" she asked nobody in particular.

"No idea," Sloan replied, barely looking up from the book she was reading. "And the Magic 8 Ball is way too far away for me to check."

"Thanks anyway," Priya said, laughing. "I can probably just wait and see. What are you reading, anyway?"

"It's a book of astrology quizzes," Sloan said. "And there's also numerology."

"Wait—is that, like, where all the numbers of your birthday get added up to tell you your fortune?" Priya thought she had seen that on a website somewhere or something once.

"Sort of," Sloan said. "But to be honest, it's kinda boring quizzing myself. Wanna take one?"

"As long as we can do it without turning on

the main lights of the tent," Priya said. "I do *not* want to get in trouble for being up past lights-out."

From her bunk, Natalie snorted. "Please. What are they going to do? Ground us from the Outdoor Adventure Weekend? I wish!"

"No, Nat—for you, they'd have a special punishment. Like, they'd make you do the boating portion in a canoe—all by yourself!" Priya said, giggling.

Natalie sighed. "Ugh, you're probably right. I am so doomed to become one with nature this summer." She flopped backward onto her bed, causing the springs to creak dramatically.

"Looks like!" Sloan chirped. "But in the meantime—quizzes!" She flicked her pink flashlight at each of the girls individually. "Who's in?"

Priya nodded happily, then watched eagerly as Natalie, Jenna, and Brynn bobbed their heads in assent. Finally, Sloan's flashlight beam lingered on Avery's pretty face. She was applying lip gloss. When she finished, she ran her fingers through her hair.

"Ick, quizzes," she said, her voice dripping with scorn. "How fun. Except not."

She popped out of her bed, revealing that she'd never changed out of her tank top and cutoff shorts from the cookout. "I'm going for a walk." She almost sounded as though she were daring the girls to stop her. Not that anyone would, even if taking a walk alone after lights-out was *way* outside of the rules of the honor code. Clearly, Avery lived above the honor code. She strode out the door abruptly without so much as a look at the other girls.

The door banged shut in her wake, leaving Priya to stare at her friends bewilderedly. "You'd think she would have had enough of walking, between the whole nature walk this morning and the hike tomorrow." She thought she'd never get used to Avery's surly demeanor.

From the corner of the room, Priya heard a stifled giggle. Its source was quickly located by Sloan's makeshift spotlight, and Priya was surprised to see Joanna sitting up in bed, biting her lip guiltily. The girl was so quiet and spent so much time in Avery's shadow that it was easy to forget that she was even in the room.

The moment she realized that she'd attracted attention, Joanna clapped a hand over her mouth, as though she was sorry she'd dared to laugh out loud. Could it be that Avery had actually trained Joanna not to *laugh*? Priya knew the girl was bad news, but seriously.

"Do you . . . want to take the quizzes with us?" Priya asked cautiously. Joanna may have lousy taste in friends, but she seemed nice enough when she was by herself. Besides, excluding her would just be plain rude, and the Lakeview girls were not rude.

Nope, that's Avery's territory, Priya thought.

For a moment the room was quiet, and Priya felt completely humiliated. Of course Joanna didn't want to take the quizzes with them. Avery thought quizzes were lame, which meant that Joanna, by default, felt exactly the same way. She should have known better than to reach out and leave herself open and feeling foolish like this.

But after a beat, Joanna cleared her throat. "Sure." She coughed, then spoke more loudly. "Yeah, sure." She sounded just as tentative as Priya had, and Priya realized that Joanna didn't know how to act around the Lakeview girls any more than they knew how to act around her. "But, um, I'm a nine."

"Huh?" A nine? Was she speaking in code?

"A nine. That's my number. For numerology." She smiled shyly and glanced in Sloan's direction. "I love numerology."

Sloan grinned. "Then you're in luck, my friend," she said, flipping her book open and uncapping her turquoise gel pen.

They hadn't gotten much further than establishing Brynn as a Leo through and through before the door burst open again and Chelsea came charging in.

"What'd I miss?" she asked, breathless. "No, wait—what did *you* miss?"

"Okay, we give. Mainly 'cause we have no idea what you're talking about," Priya said, taking in Chelsea's thick, wavy hair and thousand-watt smile with affection.

"You missed . . . *this!*" She thrust her arm into the air. In her fist she clutched a silver spoon. "Me. Kicking Assassin butt. I got Connor's spoon!"

"No *way!*" Jenna said, springing out of bed and leaping up to do an impromptu victory dance with Chelsea in the middle of the room. "You rock!

And meanwhile, how lucky are you that you got your *crush* as your target?"

"He's not my crush," Chelsea said hotly.

"Uh-huh," Priya chimed in. "Then why is your face practically about to burst into flames?"

"Well . . ." Chelsea admitted slowly. "There may have been some flirting."

"*Some* flirting?'" Natalie shrieked. The girls all shot her a warning look. Just because the counselors were in a meeting didn't mean they wouldn't hear them if everyone got too riled up. "I must hear about the flirting. I sense good gossip. *Very* good gossip. I want to know how you got the spoon," she said, whispering now.

Chelsea cast her eyes to the floor, but it was clear that she was dying to share the story of her triumph. "Well, since Justin is out of the game now, I thought he might be willing to work with me to distract Connor while I went through his stuff."

"You've never talked to Justin before in your life," Priya pointed out, admiring Chelsea's courage. Assassin had coaxed a competitive streak out of her. Or maybe just a flirtatious streak. Either way, it was working for her.

Chelsea shrugged. "Whatever. I know he's, like, *addicted* to soda. So I smuggled three cans of Coke from the cookout and brought them to him while everyone was on their way back to the tents. I explained the situation to him, and he agreed that if I came back to the tent with him, he'd distract the guys outside while I snuck in and looked around."

"What did he do to distract them?" Sloan asked.

"He told them he'd lost his iPod in the grass and that he needed their help to find it."

"That's *brilliant*," Jenna said, her voice ringing with admiration.

"I know!" Chelsea went on. "So I rushed into the tent while everyone was crawling around on the ground and poked around in Connor's cubbies. He reads *Sports Illustrated*."

"Good to know," Natalie pointed out. "Sporty. Check."

"And then, under the bed, jammed between the mattress and the bed frame . . . there it was! The spoon!" She sighed with satisfaction at the memory.

"That's all well and good," Priya said, feeling a touch jealous that Chelsea was ahead in the game, "but what about the whole flirting thing? When did *that* happen?"

"Well, when I came out of the bunk, the boys were all coming back in, and so Connor saw me—I didn't have time to dodge, or hide, or anything. And for some reason, I was afraid to tell him—like, it would hurt his feelings or something. So I told him I was there to see him!"

At this, the girls all squealed in unison.

"And he said *he was glad I came by*, and then he walked me back to our tent and we talked the whole way. And for part of it he *may* have held my hand a little." Chelsea couldn't keep the gleam from her eye, even in the semi-dark.

"So did you ever end up telling him the truth?" Priya asked.

"I had to. I mean, I couldn't just let him think he was still in the game when he wasn't. And I wasn't going to forfeit my little victory just to save his male pride," Chelsea said. "But you know what? By the time I told him the truth, the game didn't seem to matter anymore. I think we were both just happy that we got to meet each other through it."

"Awesome, Chels," Jenna said, all revved up to hear about this latest development in the game. "So, you've gotta tell us—who's your new target?"

Chelsea's mouth dropped open in indignation. "I will *not* tell you!" she retorted. "I'm ahead now. No way am I giving up my lead by oversharing with you guys. But—oh! Speaking of oversharing, I found out why Reed wasn't at the cookout tonight."

"Why?" Natalie and Brynn asked at the same time. Natalie looked extra suspicious, Priya noted. Maybe she was wondering why Brynn was taking such an interest in Reed. Priya was kind of wondering that herself.

"Well, it turns out he stepped in some poison ivy on the nature walk today, and he was too embarrassed to be seen with Calamine lotion all over his face." She wrinkled her nose. "He does look kinda pathetic and pasty."

"But, I don't understand—if he *stepped* in poison ivy, why would his *face* be rashy?" Natalie asked, confused.

"I guess when you guys sat down and he took

off his shoes, he rubbed the stuff from his feet, and then touched his face. I mean, I can't say for sure. I wasn't there. All I know is that his face looks like a helium balloon right now. I don't blame him for feeling dumb."

"Wow," Natalie said, sounding aghast.

"Oh, don't worry, Nat—it's temporary," Priya teased. "Besides, you like Reed for more than his looks, right?"

Natalie looked worried. "Yeah. Of course. But still—his looks are nice, too."

The girls dissolved in giggles, and Priya turned back to Chelsea. "We're glad you're back. We were going to have a quiz-a-palooza while Anika, Josie, and Avery are out."

"Fab idea!" Chelsea said. "Do we know where Avery is?"

"Nope," Priya said. "But we do know where Joanna is. Right here! And she's a nine. So she's going to do the quizzes with us."

"Cool," Chelsea said, sounding as though she truly meant it. She smiled at Joanna. "The more the merrier."

Quiet hour was one of the only times during the jam-packed Walla Walla daily schedule that the campers actually got a little, well . . . peace and *quiet*. Normally, Sarah preferred being outdoors and engaged in sports or some other activity, but ever since the Lakeview girls arrived at camp and the game of Assassin began, quiet hour had become one of Sarah's favorite times of the day. It was the easiest time to keep tabs on her tentmates and to make sure that they weren't getting any closer to learning her secret. It had become a routine: come back from lunch, flop down on her bunk, and pretend to read a book for forty-five minutes or so while silently keeping an eye on everyone else.

Today, however, she came back from lunch to find a surprise waiting for her. Well, not exactly waiting for *her*, really. Not really waiting for anyone in particular, but rather, trying to get in and out of the tent for some surveillance work without being spotted by anyone else.

It was Chelsea. And she was tossing Hailey's

bed like she was the tooth fairy looking for a recent deposit. The mattress was tilted up at an angle, and she was feverishly checking inside the springs of the bed frame.

"*What* are you doing?" Sarah shrieked upon seeing Chelsea tearing through the tent like it was her living room. She knew, of course, what Chelsea was doing—or at least, she had a pretty good idea— but she sort of couldn't help herself from exclaiming out loud.

She'd been dreading this moment ever since Avery had first come up with the idea of playing Assassin. And she *thought* that she had planned for it by constantly lurking and generally being obsessive about knowing where everyone was at any given time. But trying to be all-knowing that way was exhausting. A girl was bound to slip up.

That, plus, Chelsea was clearly extremely stealthy. No wonder she had slipped under Sarah's radar.

Chelsea jumped about ten feet in the air, then spun around, a guilty expression on her face. "Nothing," she said quickly. After a moment, when it became clear that Sarah wasn't buying that ruse, she went on. "Um, except that I lent a magazine to Hailey, and she told me to come back and get it if I wanted. She told me," she repeated stubbornly, as if by saying it enough times it would suddenly be true.

"Cool. Well, she should be back from lunch any second now, so, you know, you can just get it from her directly," Sarah said, challenge in her voice.

That is, if you weren't really looking for something else.

Chelsea bit her lip, looking flustered. "Right. Uh, maybe, I don't know. Maybe I'll just get it from her after dinner." She moved away from the bed and began to sidle cautiously toward the front door. Not that caution would help, Sarah thought. The cat was way out of the bag at this point.

Please, Sarah thought. Unlike the Lakeview girls, Sarah had one very particular advantage: This wasn't the first game of Assassin she'd been involved in. She knew the score.

And right about now? According to her estimations? It was pretty clear that Chelsea's new target was Hailey.

"Well, okay, anyway," Chelsea babbled, "I'm going to get going."

"Awesome," Sarah said, smirking. "I'll tell Hailey you stopped by."

"You don't have to," Chelsea mumbled. "Seriously—don't worry about it." She dashed from the tent without further ado.

Once she was gone, the smile faded from Sarah's lips. If Chelsea's new target was Hailey, then that meant that Chelsea would be spending more time around the girls from Sarah's tent— a lot more time. She'd be digging around and coming up with all sorts of stuff on Sarah and her new friends. She'd be knee-deep in their business. In their secrets.

In *Sarah's* secrets.

That wasn't going to work at all.

Sarah folded her arms across her chest and regarded the room grimly. There was no way that she could possibly let Chelsea get closer to her or to any of her friends. She was going to have to do everything she could to make sure that Chelsea was booted from the game.

And she was going to have to do it soon.

Chelsea had been on edge ever since getting busted rooting around in Hailey's tent by Sarah, of all people. She'd spent all of quiet hour gnawing on her fingernails and pretending to read the same page in *J-14* magazine over and over again. She just couldn't believe that Sarah was the one getting in her way and causing her grief. Okay, yes, Assassin was a game and they were all competing against one another, but the Sarah Chelsea had known at Lakeview wouldn't have taken so much nasty pleasure in catching her red-handed. Chelsea knew there was no way that Sarah wouldn't tell Hailey what she'd seen, and so it was up to Chelsea to make a move for Hailey's spoon as soon as she possibly could.

The question was, *how?*

She turned different ideas over in her head on her way to dinner, and rejected each one in turn. *Stage a raid so that I can rummage through Hailey's stuff while everyone else is occupied? No, we got in trouble last time we had a raid. Fake a fever so that I can stay behind while everyone else is on the Outdoor Adventure Weekend and ransack the place then? Nah, I'd probably get stuck in the infirmary, and then what? I'd miss the weekend and I still wouldn't be any closer to getting Hailey's spoon. Pull a campwide fire drill to divert everyone to the rec hall? No, that's the worst idea in the history of ever. Dr. Steve would have a conniption and then I would probably be sent home.*

Which leaves me back at square one.

"Earth to Chelsea," Sloan was saying. "Where are you?"

"Sorry, I was . . . distracted," Chelsea said, embarrassed. "I guess I just spaced out."

"Seriously," Sloan said. "You almost marched straight into Priya. You were on a collision course."

"I didn't even notice," Chelsea admitted. Since the mess hall was a safe zone, normally dinner was the one time you could let your guard down, but Chelsea's brain had gone into overdrive after she'd fled from Sarah's bunk—and Sarah's glare—earlier. And it hadn't quieted since.

As they moved to the front stairs of the mess hall, the girls were suddenly bumped from behind, sending Chelsea stumbling forward. She grabbed at Sloan's wrist to steady herself. "Whoops."

"Gosh," Sloan said. "Do people have to be so pushy about mess hall food? Mashed potatoes from a box are really not worth all of this effort."

The two girls turned around to see Sarah, a scowl fixed on her face. "Chelsea," Sarah said, pointing angrily. "What is this?"

"You, bumping into us?" Sloan suggested.

"No, I mean *this*." Sarah thrust her hand forward. Her fingers were wrapped around a spoon.

"This was in your waistband when I bumped into you. Your spoon."

Chelsea's eyes widened. "No. That's not possible. I didn't do that. I *wouldn't* do that." She didn't know where Sarah had gotten the spoon from, but she knew one thing—it was planted.

She couldn't believe what she was hearing, seeing, what Sarah was suggesting. Carrying a spoon on your person was totally against the rules! She couldn't believe that Sarah would accuse her of cheating. Sure, maybe Chelsea hadn't had the best attitude their first summer together, but since then the girls had all gotten to know one another, and Chelsea felt that her friends truly, finally, understood her.

Apparently her "friends" no longer included Sarah.

She'd known that already, of course—Sarah had made that more than apparent ever since the girls had shown up on the first day of camp—but this definitely hammered it home. Sarah had sunk to a new low. Ew. Chelsea didn't know what to make of this.

"Obviously you *would* do that and you *did* do that," Sarah said, "or I wouldn't have this spoon in my hand now, would I?" From behind Sarah, Avery snickered meanly. A small crowd had begun to form around the girls.

"If you were caught cheating, you're automatically disqualified," Avery said. "It's the rules."

"Great. Except *Chelsea didn't cheat*," Sloan said loudly.

"Are you saying I'm a liar?" Sarah asked, her voice laced with challenge.

"Actually—" Sloan started.

"Forget it," Chelsea said, cutting her off. Obviously Chelsea knew that Chelsea hadn't cheated. And Sarah knew that Chelsea hadn't cheated. And Sarah knew that Chelsea knew that Sarah knew Chelsea hadn't cheated. Which, in addition to being extremely confusing, meant that Sarah was willing to fight dirty to get Chelsea knocked out of the game.

It made no sense. The Sarah she'd known at Lakeview was a good sport, fair, honest.

Then again, the Sarah she'd known at Lakeview was also *nice*.

This Sarah was different. *Way* different.

And not, Chelsea decided, worth her energy any longer.

"Just forget about it," she said again, frustrated. "I'm out. I'm done with the game, and I don't care."

It wasn't true, of course. Of *course* she cared about the game—as well as what the other campers thought of her. But there was nothing to be done about that now, was there? So she simply ran ahead to the mess hall without waiting to hear what anyone else had to say.

EIGHT

Dear Lacy,

I send this letter under the threat of mortal danger.

Okay, just kidding, but oh . . . my . . . gosh, have things gotten crazy around here—crazier than things ever get at school—ever since we all started playing Assassin.

As I write this, three of my fellow tentmates are completely MIA: Natalie, Jenna, and Brynn. I'd give you three guesses what they're doing, but I bet you won't need more than one. Obvs they're out on some kind of information-gathering/ strategizing weirdness, possibly tunneling through the camp via underground passageway, or fashioning magnifying lenses from the nature shack into periscopes. Who even knows?

Not that I don't have Assassin fever—trust me, it rubs off—but all of that competitiveness and aggression is bad for your aura. And also your skin. So I'm taking the game to a kinder, gentler level.

(And drinking lots of water. Hydration is important.)

Besides, you might be surprised by how much a person can uncover simply by keeping quiet and keeping her ears open.

Or maybe you wouldn't. Be surprised, I mean. You always were a slightly sneaky one, huh?

What else? Well, crazy, camp-wide, high-stakes (or, er, medium-stakes, anyway), head-trippy games aside, the other big news around here is the Outdoor Adventure Weekend, which officially kicks off Friday morning. Yay.

(If you think you're sensing sarcasm there, then you think right. Way right.)

The thing is that, coming from Sedonah, it's not that I don't like the outdoors. I mean, you know I love the annual green fair that our school puts on in the tents behind the community center. But there's a huge difference between eco-living out in the desert and rafting, boating, paddling . . . basically, anything involving a body of water. Just popping on a life preserver is kind of enough of an "adventure" for me, and I'm not enough of a thrill-seeker to want to "take it up a notch," as Jenna keeps encouraging.

I don't know. Maybe I'm just a party pooper. Don't get me wrong—I know it'll be fun. I just wish it weren't three whole days of "fun" in store. And that Avery didn't have to be there with us.

Correction: Avery and her smirk. Which always seem to travel together. Yuck.

She hasn't gotten any nicer, by the way. Just in case you were wondering.

I have no idea who has her as a

target, but whoever it is, I hope she gets her takedown, but good—not to put bad karma out there, but man, would it be nice to have her get a little bit of a taste of her own medicine. Besides, she was the one who began the game, anyway, so maybe it actually is karma—like, for her, I mean.

Who knows? There's something about that girl. Despite the fact that she has decided that we Lakeview girlies aren't worthy of her friendship, she herself always seems to come out on top, no matter what happens.

Don't you just hate people like that?

Well, I'd better go. If I put any-more negativity out there into the world, karma will come and kick my butt, right? Right.

I knew you'd see it my way.

Anyways, we have an "outdoor skills refresher course" demonstration thingy happening any second. I can tell because Jenna's back, and she's bouncing up and down by the door of the tent like she's got springs attached to the soles of her sneakers.

Enthusiasm. It's cute. I think I'll go find Nat so there's someone to sit with in the back row.

(If only there were a happy medium somewhere in between Jenna and Natalie's excitement levels. Or . . . I guess maybe that's Priya?)

Though, maybe it could come in handy knowing how to pitch a tent, boil down rainwater to purify it, and identify edible bugs in case of an emergency.

Just kidding about that bug thing. I HOPE.

xoxo.

Your (soon-to-be majorly adventurous) friend,

Sloan

"In preparation for your Outdoor Adventure Weekend, Neeks and I are going to be showing you a few camping basics," Tucker explained, pacing back and forth energetically in front of the campers assembled in the Walla Walla rec room. Standing beside him, Anika grinned and gave everyone a big thumbs-up. Jackson stood behind them both, pointing at different pieces of equipment like a game show host whenever Tucker or Anika indicated. He caught Jenna's eye and winked. The two of them had bonded over Jenna's enthusiasm for ropes. Especially since none of her other Lakeview friends really shared it.

Jenna winked back at the C.I.T . She was *all over* this demo. She'd been camping a bunch—before her parents divorced, the Blooms had done an annual trip to the Adirondacks—but she had a feeling that a Walla Walla camping weekend would be an entirely unique experience.

"First things first," Tucker said, ticking off on his hand as he counted, "you want to pitch your tent on *level ground*."

Jackson held his arms out in a T, doing a dramatization of "level."

Next to Jenna, Avery snorted. Jenna ignored her. *Level ground—check*, she thought, creating a mental list for herself to refer to over the course of the weekend.

"Next, you want to check and make sure that there's a water source nearby," Tucker went on. "Now, we're going to be hiking along the edge of the water, so that won't be a problem, but it's still something that you should keep in mind. There's a *reason*, after all, that we're hiking along the water. Technically, more than one reason."

Now Avery sighed, as though the whole demonstration were just too boring to endure for another moment.

Jackson shot Avery a look and she flushed, sitting straighter in her seat. Jenna observed this exchange with curiosity—could it be true? Was there actually someone in camp who had a quieting effect on Avery and her endless black cloud of snide remarks and sarcasm? Interesting. She'd have to keep an eye on that.

"So," Anika jumped in, "what are some other things to look for when choosing a campsite?"

Jenna reached her hand in the air, but not before she saw Avery lean over to Joanna, whisper something in her ear, and begin to snicker.

Whatever Jackson's effect on Avery, it wasn't enough to reform her completely. The girl obviously just couldn't help herself.

What is her problem? Jenna wondered. The attitude was not fun to deal with. Not at all.

Thankfully, Avery had finally managed to attract some attention other than Jenna and Jackson. Anika whipped her head around and looked at the smirking girl.

"Yes, Avery? I take it you have the answer, or you wouldn't be chatting with Joanna?"

Since the remark hadn't come from Jackson, Avery wasn't chastened at all. In fact, Jenna noted, she *rolled her eyes* before answering Anika. "You want to check for shade, you want to find a place for cooking, and you have to find a separate place for disposing of garbage."

Anika looked resigned to the fact that at least Avery had gotten the answer right. "Yes. Disposal of trash is really important, since doing it improperly could attract animals, not to mention harm the environment. But Avery—" she added— "just because this information is stuff that you already know doesn't mean that you can talk while we're giving a demonstration."

Avery widened her eyes into an innocent expression. "It's not just me and Joanna, Anika," she insisted. "*Everyone* knows this stuff. I mean, it's, like, camping 101."

Just another not-so-subtle dig at the Lakeview girls, Jenna thought.

Anika looked as though she were considering how to reply to this, but Tucker clearly decided that the best thing to do was just to plow ahead. "How about you humor us, Avery, just in case?" he suggested. "Now we'll show you all how to pitch a tent. Jackson will be there to help us over the weekend, but I personally would feel better knowing that you'd given the demo your full attention."

At the mention of Jackson's name, Avery beamed and looked much more interested again. "Of course," she said, contrite.

"Great!" Tucker looked incredibly relieved. "Okay, then—what we've got here is all of the equipment for your standard four-person tent. Can I get a volunteer to help me put this together up here while everyone watches?"

Jenna stretched as far forward as her body would bend. She was dying for a chance to put a tent together herself, without her parents, Stephanie, Adam, or anyone else to get in the way. This would be sort of like a rite of passage.

"Perfect—Jenna," Tucker said, nodding in her direction.

Yes! she thought, skipping up toward the front of the room.

Surveying the crowd, she could see that David was also clamoring to be picked. That would be fun. Jenna and David had always worked well together in anything teamwork oriented. That was probably why they had been good together as a couple, but were also great friends.

"David," Tucker said. "Hmm . . ." he pointed. "And Reed."

Reed looked surprised, but he got up and joined the group up front without argument.

This'll be good, Jenna thought. Reed was, like, the least outdoorsy person in the whole camp.

Then again, she realized, *that's probably why Tucker chose him.*

At the mention of Reed's name, Natalie's hand shot up, reminding Jenna of who the *second* least outdoorsy person in the whole camp was. Jenna knew the only reason Nat was volunteering was for the chance to work with Reed.

Before Tucker could call on Nat, though, Brynn called out. "Me! Me!" she shouted, waving her hands like an air traffic controller. Her red curls bounced as she stretched her neck forward.

There was no way to ignore her, and Tucker didn't even try. "How can I say no to *that?*" Tucker laughed, waving her up to the front. "Come on, Brynn. Help us out!"

Brynn sprang to her feet and jogged up to the front. Once she got there, she shot a small, secretive smile at Reed.

Jenna caught their exchange with surprise. What was Brynn doing trying to get closer to Natalie's guy? Especially when she had Jordan? Was Jenna imagining things?

One glance at Natalie told her that her eyes weren't playing tricks on her—that whatever she'd seen, Natalie had seen it, too. And wasn't happy about it.

Jenna bit her lip, worried. She had no idea what was going on with Brynn, but it didn't look good. The Lakeview girls hadn't exactly been embraced with open arms since arriving at Walla Walla. It wasn't like they could afford to let their own friendships dissolve.

But if Brynn kept up this weird flirting with Natalie's boy, that was *exactly* what was going to happen.

chapter

NINE

"Last one on the bus is a rotten egg!"

Chelsea looked up to see Jenna hanging off the bottom step of one of two school buses that would take them to the campsite. The school buses, which had been packed to the gills with camping gear, were nearly ready, Chelsea realized with a start, to take them off into the great unknown.

Gulp.

Natalie sidled up to her and elbowed her in the ribs. "Do you think there's something slightly off about them having to *drive* us to a *hiking* site?"

Chelsea had to laugh. "Would you rather that they made us walk all the way there? Something tells me we'll be getting plenty of exercise soon enough. Besides, I'd rather not be loaded down with gear until the last possible minute."

Natalie nodded. "Sometimes you are extremely wise."

Chelsea smiled. "Only sometimes?"

"Are you guys coming?" Jenna hollered from the bus, saving Natalie the trouble of having to answer.

"Why don't you save us seats?" Chelsea suggested, savoring her last few moments of pre-Outdoor Adventure innocence.

It's all uphill from here, she thought to herself nervously. *Probably even literally!*

Almost as if he'd overheard her private thoughts, Dr. Steve stepped in front of the first bus, clipboard in hand and vocal chords at the ready.

"I came by to see you all off!" he exclaimed. He looked, Chelsea noted, extremely chipper at the prospect of sending a bunch of young people off into the woods to fend for themselves.

At least that means they probably haven't lost any campers on one of these weekends—yet.

The thought wasn't much of a consolation.

"I know you're going to have a great time—and learn a lot!"

Doesn't he know that camp is not for learning? Camp is the opposite of learning! Camp is what you do in the summer, when you're not in school! Chelsea felt quite certain of that, and in fact made a solemn vow right then and there to do as little overt learning as possible over the weekend in particular, and the summer in general.

Suddenly she heard a voice in her ear. "Isn't the summer for *fun*, not 'learning'?"

She turned to find Connor grinning at her, making little air quote signs with his hands as he said the word "learning." Clearly he felt the same way about all of this as she did.

Chelsea wasn't exactly the swooning type. But still, this was a moment that could call for a swoon.

She decided to compromise—a mini-swoon. On the inside.

On the outside, she smiled at Connor. (This smiling thing was really working out for her these days; she couldn't believe she'd taken as long as she had to come around to the friendlier side of life.) "I have a feeling we're going to be 'learning,' this weekend, whether we like it or not," she proclaimed. "The Clipboard has spoken."

Connor laughed out loud. Chelsea decided that she loved that sound. "Who are we to deny The Clipboard?" Connor asked. "Who knows? Maybe it'll be fun." He paused for a moment, looking as if he were deep in thought. "Do you want to sit with me on the bus?"

Did she? Chelsea had to press her lips together to keep from squealing. Jenna wouldn't mind, she knew—there'd be someone else to take the space that Jenna had saved for her. Besides, her friends were constantly encouraging her to spend more time with Connor. They were way into the idea of Chelsea and Connor as a couple.

Forget The Clipboard—who was she to deny her *friends*?

"Yeah, definitely," Chelsea said, trying not to smile so widely that her cheeks split. "Cool."

The weekend was starting to look up, that was for sure. Maybe Dr. Steve was right—maybe she *was* going to have a great time, after all.

She crossed her fingers as she and Connor boarded the bus, just to be safe.

Brynn could barely breathe.

She could barely breathe, and what was worse, she couldn't believe there had ever been a time when an afternoon on the ropes course would have seemed like a walk in the park.

But the ropes course? That was then. And the monster Outdoor Adventure Weekend kickoff hike? *That* was now.

A *hike*. In the *woods*. Not a walk in the park at all.

Just like she had on the ropes course, Brynn tried to channel her inner actress, to imagine herself playing a role. To see the movie image of herself in her mind and make it feel a little bit less "now" and intense.

The problem with that approach was that it didn't get her from point A to point B any faster, or make the ground any more level or less overgrown. It certainly didn't do anything about the swarm of gnats that had decided to make the back of Brynn's neck their own personal dance floor.

Besides, if this were a movie, she'd *totally* have a stunt double. So she wouldn't have to do any imagining or removing herself from the now. That would be the stunt double's job.

Why couldn't they have stunt doubles for their Outdoor Adventure Weekend? It would be so much easier that way.

"Note the low-hanging branches on the side of the path," Anika was saying, indicating some spindly-looking twigs that Brynn kept having to duck from in order to keep them from smacking her in the forehead.

Path? Brynn wondered. All she could see in front of her was the slimmest break in the dense, leafy floor of the forest. It was barely better than a trail of breadcrumbs.

And everybody knew what happened to kids in fairy tales who followed bread crumbs . . .

Which reminded her—she couldn't afford to fall behind. She'd never find her way to the campsite on her own.

"The reason the branches are bare is because local wildlife have eaten all of the leaves. That's how we know that these woods are populated with deer and other animals." Anika sounded pleased as punch about the idea of all sorts of wild creatures wandering around the wide open space that they were going to be calling their bedroom for the evening.

Brynn, less so.

"And you can see from the muddier clumps here and there that we're getting closer to our water source—"

If Brynn had been paying better attention, rather than swatting at a particularly aggressive insect, she might have noticed that *here* and *there* were actually, in point of fact, *right there*. Right in front of her. Slippery, wet, muddy clumps.

Unfortunately, she was too caught up in regretting not having used stronger bug repellent to take note of that tiny detail.

Which meant that the next step that she took. . .

. . . landed her squarely in the middle of a thick patch—or *clump*, per Anika's extremely specific nature talk—of ishy, squishy mud.

"Whoa—" she started as she slid forward, but it was too late.

Brynn was going down.

She landed with a *splat*, splashing mud up and over her legs, her upper body, her face, her hair . . . basically everywhere. She was *covered* in mud.

Up until this point in the hike, Brynn had basically been trying to be a good sport about the whole thing. The bug bites, the heat, the pebbles on the ground that made her ankles turn in different directions when she least expected it . . . Yeah, she'd dealt with all of those. She'd kept her gripes mostly on the inside. But now?

Now she had mud dripping down her back and possibly creeping over the waistband of her shorts.

This was a full-contact, mud-on-skin situation. *Gross.*

The time for a positive attitude had long since passed.

Brynn made a decision. She took a deep breath and screamed.

Anika immediately rushed over. "Brynn, are you okay?" she asked, concern etched across her features as she kneeled on the ground.

Brynn couldn't help but notice that Anika didn't seem to have any qualms whatsoever about plunking herself right down in the mud. Suddenly, she felt extremely foolish. Also, her throat was raw from that mondoshriek that she'd unleashed.

"Um, I fell," she said. She reached up and tried to brush a strand of hair out of her eyes, but only succeeded in painting a streak of mud across her forehead.

"Yeah, I can see that," Anika said, still sounding very worried. "What did you hurt?"

It dawned on Brynn that there was a reason that most people, people who'd been trained in outdoorsy type experiences, didn't go around freaking out every time they took a skid, or tripped, or fell over. It was because screaming *worried* people. It made them think you'd broken something. Or that you needed special attention or first aid or something serious, rather than that you were just kind of unused to nature in such huge quantities, and maybe didn't enjoy the sensation of mud on the inside of your waistband, and were possibly wishing that your knapsack held an extra change of clean clothes.

"I'm . . . fine," she admitted slowly. "I think I was just, uh, taken by surprise, you know? 'Cause I slipped, and I went down, like, right away, and I didn't even see the mud patch." Her cheeks were flaming red and she was wishing she'd just pulled herself up and dusted herself off without making such a huge production out of her surfin' safari. At this point other campers had begun to gather and were taking in the scene with a mixture of bewilderment and amusement.

"Gosh, are you always such a drama queen?" Hailey asked, her face folding into a sneer.

"I . . . maybe," Brynn stammered, at a loss. "Yeah, I guess so."

"It's okay, Brynn," Anika said warmly, rising and extending a firm arm to help Brynn pull herself up. "We've all been caught off guard on a hike before. But that's why it's so important to keep one eye on the ground, no matter how distracted you are by the beauty of your surroundings."

She wasn't even kidding. She thought Brynn had been all distracted by *beauty* and *happiness* and leaves and raindrops and cheery rays of sunshine.

Now Brynn felt like the biggest party pooper of all time.

"Right, of course," she said dully. The beauty of her surroundings. Ha! All she'd been distracted by was the itching on the back of her neck and the earliest signs of pre-lunch hunger pangs.

Sigh.

She was beginning to suspect that she *really* wasn't cut out for any sort of Outdoor Adventure.

Clearly, she wasn't the only one who thought as much. Hailey was still staring at her in total disbelief.

"Seriously, Brynn," she was saying. "You'd think that *you* were the one with the acting genes in your family. Try taking it down a notch—for the rest of our sakes."

Satisfied that she'd spread enough nastiness for the moment, Hailey turned on one heel and trotted off to catch up with her friends who were farther ahead, leaving Brynn dumbfounded.

"Do you have acting genes in your family?" Anika asked, much calmer and friendlier now that it was clear that Brynn was still in one piece.

"No," Brynn said, shaking her head in wonder. "Not me." Hailey's words echoed in her head.

You'd think that you were the one with the acting genes in your family.

But she *wasn't.*

Natalie was the one with the acting genes in her family, of course. *Natalie* was the one with the famous father. Not Brynn.

But Natalie had been keeping the information about her father a secret. She'd wanted to get to know the people at Walla Walla without having to wonder if they were only interested in her because her father was Tad Maxwell.

But Hailey seemed to know something. Which meant that now Brynn had to wonder—was Natalie's secret out? And if so, who had let the cat out of the bag?

Had Hailey found out about Tad Maxwell while playing Assassin? Had someone else found out and spread the rumor around?

Did *everyone* know?

Brynn was worried. She knew Natalie would be totally upset to know that rumors were going around about how her father was famous. Brynn crossed her fingers and hoped that, for Natalie's sake, she'd somehow misunderstood what Hailey was getting at.

Although—she had to admit—it didn't seem likely. Unfortunately.

⛺ ⛺ ⛺

After an agonizing hike up to the lake, and a night spent sleeping on dirt, Priya was pleasantly surprised to find that—who knew?—she actually kind of *liked* fishing.

The experience was unexpectedly zen, from the methodical procedure for baiting the line (she made Jordan—whom she had borrowed from Brynn for the afternoon—deal with the worm, of course, which just seemed fair. Boys liked worms and things, right?) and sending it out into the water, to the ripples that fanned out in the line's wake. In the early afternoon, the sun was bright but not unbearable, and a breeze came off of the surface of the lake, tickling Priya's shoulders. She hunkered down on a cluster of rocks, appreciating the chance to give her burning leg muscles a rest.

Mind you, she still had *no idea* what she would do if she actually caught anything—she'd probably just get Jordan to throw it back—but for now, she was perfectly content.

"This could be worse," she admitted, turning to Jordan with a smile.

"That's because you got me to do your dirty work," he reminded her. He tugged lightly at his line and watched his lure bob up and down for a beat or two.

"Yeah," she agreed, "but you're a boy. You like grossness like worms and other creepy crawly things."

He laughed. "Fair enough. But you owe me."

"I can live with that. The next time you need help with something girly and non-creepy-crawly, I'm there for ya." Her stomach rumbled briefly, disrupting her train of thought. "I'm hungry. What do you think is for lunch?"

He tilted his head in the direction of the lake. "Well, what have you caught?"

Priya made a face. "No. No *way* am I eating a fish that we caught ourselves. I mean, I like sushi as much as anyone, but the worms and the bait were bad enough. I refuse to clean a fish or anything like that."

Jordan shrugged. "I think it'd be cool to eat something we caught ourselves. But I hear you. And I'm not sure that Tucker would want us to be fooling around with knives and whatever else it takes to filet something."

"Good," Priya said with finality. "Maybe we'll get some PB&J or something, then."

"This is an *Outdoor Adventure Weekend*," Jordan teased her. "You are not being very ad—"

He was cut off suddenly by the sound of cheering. Priya tilted her body, craning her neck over her shoulder and trying to see what was going on.

It was Sarah, waving two spoons in the air. "These were in one of the tackle boxes," she called out. "Whose are they? You're out." She rolled her eyes. "Seriously guys—the tackled boxes? While we're fishing? How did you think that you weren't going to get caught?"

Molly and Caitlyn, two girls from Sarah's bunk, stepped forward, looking abashed. "It was ours," Molly said. "We teamed up to come up with a good hiding spot," Caitlyn added.

Sarah snickered. "And *this* was your big idea?"

Molly nodded. "We thought it was Tucker's box. So that he'd be the only one looking in it."

"You thought wrong," Sarah trilled. She looked around, surveying the group. "Looks like I inherit your targets." She folded her arms across her chest with satisfaction. "Looks like I'm kicking tail in this game."

It sure does look that way, Priya thought, turning back to her holding pattern with the fishing reel now that the drama had died down a little bit. Sarah was definitely rushing full steam ahead in this game. The girls even suspected that she'd planted a spoon on Chelsea in an effort to cheat the other day, even though Chelsea had begged off and refused to discuss the matter.

Priya had no idea why this was all so important to Sarah.

Then again, there were a lot of things about Sarah that Priya—and the others—really didn't know anymore.

chapter TEN

"Sloan, did you bring your tarot cards?"

Sloan looked up from the charred marshmallow that she'd been contemplating to find Chelsea regarding her hopefully. She swallowed the last bite of sticky-sweet goodness and licked her fingertips clean. "Sorry, nope. I was trying to pack light." Seeing as how they were expected to carry their packs all on their own and everything. As much as she *loved* doing tarot readings, the deck just didn't seem like a "must."

"Pfft." Chelsea blew a raspberry, visibly disappointed. "Nat doesn't have any magazines, either. What are we going to do?"

The campers were all huddled around a massive fire pit that Tucker, Jackson, and Anika had built, relaxing after a feast of hot dogs, chips, soda, and, of course, roasted marshmallows. The pig-out session was seriously welcome after such a long and high-octane day. Sloan was feeling full, sleepy, and satisfied. But she had to admit that magazines, cards, or some other form of entertainment would have been a welcome cap to the evening.

She tilted her head back and took in the star-studded sky. It reminded her of a trip she'd once taken to a planetarium when she was younger. The lights had gone out, and the domed ceiling had exploded in pinpricks of glitter. It was nothing like the sky she saw when she went to bed at night back home, in the suburbs. This sky looked just like that. She didn't know nature could be so . . . vivid. She felt like she could see each and every individual star hovering above, winking directly at her.

She winked back and popped another marshmallow on her stick.

Maybe there were some upsides to Outdoor CORE, after all.

"Um, we could do palm readings," she suggested, having a sudden wave of inspiration. Palm readings didn't require any extra equipment or anything like that.

"Oooh, fun!" Natalie exclaimed. She scooted closer to where Sloan sat and thrust her palm out in front of Sloan's face. "Me first!"

The rest of the girls gathered around eagerly. Even Sarah's tentmates edged closer, although reluctantly and feigning nonchalance.

"Where did you learn how to read palms?" Joanna asked, not looking at Avery as she moved in toward the group.

Not that Avery would have noticed, anyway. From the corner of her eye, Sloan could see her pelting Jackson with marshmallows. For his part, Jackson appeared to be trying very hard to be good-natured about the marshmallow attack.

Better him than any of the girls. The only thing more annoying than a nasty Avery, it seemed, was a hyper, playful Avery.

Ugh. Pass. Sloan didn't want that.

"My aunt in New Mexico is a psychic healer," Sloan explained, ignoring Avery's giggle. "She's taught me lots of stuff. I can do tarot, palm reading, zodiac charts, auras . . ."

"She's basically a New Age one-stop shop," Natalie quipped. She wiggled her fingers in front of Sloan's face again. "So come on—tell, tell, tell!"

Sloan chuckled and lifted Natalie's palm closer to her face. She studied each line, every crease, thinking hard as she watched shadows from the fire dance their way across the surface of Nat's skin.

"Ooh, look at that," she said. "Your love line is thick. It's very strong!"

"Really?" Natalie squealed, stealing a glance over toward where Reed was goofing off with David, Jordan, and some of the other boys.

"Really," Sloan said. "Except—I think it's a guy back home."

Natalie looked alarmed.

"It's just—I see the New York City skyline, you know? Here." She pointed to the fleshy curve just underneath Natalie's thumb. "And there's . . . ooh, fanciness!"

Natalie's eyebrow arched, as Sloan knew it would. Natalie may not have liked the news that she and Reed weren't necessarily True Love Forever, but she did love an excuse to get fancy.

"Maybe it's a school formal?" Sloan suggested. "And you're going to get all done up? Oh—I know! You can wear your Oscar dress!" She was referring to the spectacular gown that Natalie had worn when her father had taken her to the Oscars last year, of course.

Avery's ears perked up, and she abandoned her marshmallows. She didn't waste a second to pounce. She sneered. "*Oscar* dress? Is that, like, your dorky nickname for your good clothes? Please." Now she full-on snorted. "You should talk to Sarah about Oscar dresses. Her father took her to the ceremonies last year. So *she* would know all of the fashion dos and don'ts."

Sloan's jaw dropped open, and Natalie's arm fell limply at her side. The girls exchanged stunned glances. *What* had Sarah been telling all of her friends from Walla Walla?

Suddenly Sloan understood why Hailey had made that weird comment to Brynn about having dramatic genes in the family, and why Joanna had talked about Sarah's secret. All at once, everything fell into place.

Sarah's secret was *Natalie's* secret.

Sloan had no idea why, but obviously, when Sarah first arrived at Camp Walla Walla, she'd lied to all of the other campers and told them that her father was a famous movie star. She'd basically stolen Natalie's life story and tried to pass it off as her own.

Sloan was shocked. Why would anyone do something like that? She couldn't possibly have thought that she would be able to keep people from uncovering her lies. Or that Natalie would ever forgive her for something like this.

Maybe Sarah thought that was the only way to impress people, the only way she could make new friends. According to Natalie and Jenna, she'd always been a little bit shy and insecure, after all.

But Sloan couldn't feel too sorry for Sarah; not only had she lied to them all, but she'd pushed the Lakeview girls away ever since they first arrived at camp!

Of course, now Sloan understood why Sarah couldn't be friends with them anymore—if Avery, Joanna, or any of Sarah's new friends got to know Natalie and the rest of them, they'd figure out Sarah's lies. Which would leave Sarah back at square one—or worse.

No wonder Sarah was playing Assassin so aggressively—she didn't want the Walla Walla girls getting closer to the Lakeview girls, or vice versa.

Sarah had basically painted herself into a corner. It would have been sad, if she hadn't sold her old friends out in the process.

Sloan caught Natalie's eye and realized right away that Nat had put two and two together, as well. They both glanced at Sarah to find her shooting them a pleading look. Sloan understood immediately that Sarah was begging them not to give her away.

Sloan sighed. *Fine*, she thought, *I won't say anything.* It was a weird situation, and the last thing she needed was to get caught in the middle of it. Not to mention, she had no good reason to make things rough for Sarah, even though Sarah certainly hadn't gone easy on any of them.

It wasn't Sarah's secret, anyway; it was Natalie's. And Natalie wanted to keep it that way. So maybe it was better just to let Sarah's friends believe her wild stories, for now. It was Natalie's choice, in any case.

Thoughts flew through Sloan's mind at the speed of sound. She was more than ready to curl up in her sleeping bag and call it a night. She had no idea what to make of any of this new information. The only thing that she—and her friends—could be sure of now was that Sarah was not to be trusted.

Natalie was dreaming. She knew it was a dream, because in it she was at the Oscars, watching from the bleachers as Sarah walked down the red carpet on the arm of Tad Maxwell, *Natalie's* father, not Sarah's, wearing the dress that *Natalie* had rocked when she had gone to the Oscars in real life.

Flashbulbs popped and Sarah waved and struck pose after pose as Tad smiled at her and looked on approvingly.

No! Natalie wanted to scream. *This isn't happening! No matter how much Sarah wishes it were.*

She woke with a start to realize that someone *was* screaming. In real life. Loudly.

She sat up in her sleeping bag, awake at once. Bloodcurdling shrieks in the dead of night had a tendency to do that to a person. "What's going on?"

"No idea," Jenna said, eyes darting back and forth and clearly trying to adjust to the light. "Someone's losing it."

"Thanks, oh brilliant detective," Nat said sarcastically.

"It's coming from the direction of the boys' sleeping bags," Jenna said.

Natalie's eyes flew open. "It's coming from *Reed's* sleeping bag!" she realized, rushing over to see what was wrong.

She wasn't the first to arrive, however. When she got there, David was holding a small green snake and trying—unsuccessfully—to calm Reed down.

"It's just a garter snake," David said, speaking in low, even tones. "Tucker pointed out a bunch of them while we made our way to the campsite this afternoon. They're totally harmless."

"*Not* when they creep into your sleeping bag while you're asleep!" Reed shuddered. "Ugh, I can't even look at it."

Natalie patted him on the shoulder. "It's pretty gross," she agreed. The idea of waking up to a snake inside her sleeping bag did not appeal.

Inside, however, she had to wonder if maybe Reed was overreacting just a little bit. Not that she wouldn't have been completely freaked out to wake up to find a snake in her sleeping bag, but Reed was . . . a boy. And as much as Nat was all about girl power, she did somewhere, in the very back of her mind, think that boys were supposed to be men about things like snakes and other ickiness.

Like how Jordan had baited Priya's line for her while fishing that afternoon. Jordan didn't strike Natalie as the type of guy to lose it if he came across a slithery reptile by surprise.

Which, in turn, made Natalie wonder just what her "type" of guy really was.

She was starting to think that maybe Reed wasn't "the one."

She gave Reed a quick hug and went back to her own sleeping bag, hoping she'd be able to fall back asleep. It had been a long day, and she knew they would need their rest for the hike back the next morning.

As she settled back in, she felt a tap on her shoulder. She looked up to find Avery hovering over her, looking smug.

"I guess your boyfriend's not so tough, huh?" Avery asked. Her mouth turned up at the corners, making her look especially mean.

I guess your friend Sarah isn't . . . Natalie didn't even allow herself to finish that thought—there was no point in getting herself all riled up about the Sarah situation, especially since there was nothing she could do about it without outing her secret in the process.

"I like sensitive guys," Natalie said, turning her attention back to the here and now. She glared at Avery, annoyed that the girl had managed to pick up on a truth that Natalie herself was trying to avoid.

"Uh-huh. Sure you do," Avery said. She stalked off.

Natalie curled back up into her sleeping bag, zipping it closed up to her neck. She closed her eyes and thought about what Avery had said.

And she wished that it wasn't a little bit true.

$$\blacktriangle \quad \blacktriangle \quad \blacktriangle$$

"So, okay, truth time," David was saying. "Impressions of Outdoor Adventure Weekend? Now that we're rounding the finish line?"

Jenna smiled as she hiked along next to her onetime boyfriend, now friend. Things felt very easy and comfortable with David, and even if she wasn't still crushing on him, it was good to know that they were as close as ever, friends-wise. Jenna knew that they were meant to be friends rather than crushes to each other, which was nice.

"Truth," she said, pondering his question. "Okay, well, it was definitely fun. I mean, hard, and I learned a lot, but I liked it. I like learning hard things, you know?"

David smiled. "That's my Jenna. Always up for a challenge."

Jenna blushed and tucked a strand of hair behind her ear. "What can I say? I was the one who was psyched to come to Camp Walla Walla this year, remember?"

"How could I forget?" David smiled. "You were, like, the only one of us who was."

She frowned at him teasingly. "Are you telling me you're sorry that you came with us? I mean, you learned how to purify water, and how to tell about different kinds of insects just based on the sort of tunnels and holey things that they leave in the dirt . . ."

". . . a talent that will really come in handy when I get back home," David finished wryly.

"Fine. Be a spoilsport. You're not going to ruin my good time." Jenna couldn't remember the last time she'd woken feeling so refreshed—something about the outdoor air was better than the world's strongest sugar rush—and she wasn't the least bit bothered by David's tempered enthusiasm. She turned to him, stuck her tongue out, and crossed her eyes for good measure.

The sound of Tucker's whistle brought their conversation to a halt, and they rushed forward to gather around where Tucker stood, surrounded by the rest of the campers.

"Guys, we're coming up on the kayaking leg of our trip," he explained. "And while, as you know, kayaks are one person per boat, we're going to team up with buddies so that everyone is accountable to someone else. No matter what, you must have your buddy in sight at all times until we dock farther downstream. Does that make sense?"

Jenna nodded to herself, even though Tucker wasn't talking directly to her or anything. She glanced quickly at Natalie to see who she'd be buddying with, and wasn't surprised to see Natalie checking out Reed with curiosity for what she assumed was the same reason.

Then something happened that *did* surprise Jenna. Big-time.

Natalie stepped forward, obviously planning to ask Reed if he wanted to pair up, when Brynn suddenly popped up and intercepted him.

"Hey, Reed," Brynn said, sticking her hands in the pockets of her jean shorts and trying, Jenna thought, to look very casual. "Want to be my buddy?"

Reed wrinkled his forehead and shot a quick glance at Natalie over Brynn's shoulder. Jenna watched as Natalie widened her eyes and shrugged. Obviously she had no idea what Brynn was doing, either. But she didn't make a big thing out of it, which kind of meant that Reed's kayaking partner had basically been decided for him.

"Um, sure. Yeah," he said, looking at Brynn with confusion.

For her part, Brynn completely ignored whatever awkwardness was radiating out of Reed. "Great!" she chirped. "We'll catch up downstream!" She scampered off, leaving a very puzzled Natalie and Reed in her wake.

Jenna bit her lip and threw another sympathetic glance toward her friend. She didn't know what to make of Brynn's behavior, and neither did Natalie, clearly.

Maybe it's something in the water at Camp Walla

Walla, Jenna mused. *First Sarah, now Brynn. Everyone is acting all kinds of crazy these days . . .*

▲ ▲ ▲

Okay, Natalie thought. *Enough is enough. I need to get to the bottom of this.*

She really really *really* didn't think that Brynn was the type of girl to cheat on her boyfriend and flirt with a friend's crush, but what other explanation could there be for her sudden interest in Reed? It didn't make any sense. And Natalie knew she wasn't the only one who had noticed what was going on—the look that Jenna had given her moments ago confirmed that she wasn't imagining things. As much as she may have wished that she were.

First Sarah was co-opting Natalie's life story, and now Brynn was after her boyfriend. Had everyone in her life gone nuts?

"Brynn," she said, clearing her throat awkwardly. "Um, can I talk to you before we get in the kayaks?"

"Of course," Brynn said brightly. "What's going on?"

"It's just . . ." Natalie waved Brynn over and behind a big, leafy tree so that they could have some privacy. "Okay, I don't know how to say this, so I'm just going to come out and say it. What's the deal with you and Reed?"

Brynn's brow furrowed in confusion. "What do you mean?"

Natalie sighed. "What do I mean? I mean, the

way that you've been stuck on him like glue! Do you, like, *like* him or something? 'Cause if you do, I wish you would tell me honestly."

Realization dawned in Brynn's eyes. "Oooh. I could see why you might think that."

"Really?" Natalie asked dryly. "You can see that?" A blind person could have seen that!

"It's not how it looks, Nat," Brynn insisted. "I—" she leaned forward. "Can you keep a secret?"

Natalie eyed her warily. "A *Reed* secret? Why would you have Reed secrets?" She was full-on exasperated by now.

Brynn burst out laughing and cupped a hand over Natalie's ear and whispered something. After a moment, Natalie started laughing, too.

She still didn't know what on earth was going on with Sarah. But for now, one mystery was solved. So that was something.

ELEVEN

Priya would have thought that after a crazy-long weekend of outdoor adventuring, her division would have been given a day or two to just chill out and relax. That way, maybe she and her friends could lounge around their tents and read, give one another manicures, or hang out by the waterfront perfecting their tans.

She would have thought that, but she would have been wrong.

On Monday afternoon, the girls were back at the waterfront, all right. But they sure weren't sunbathing.

No. Not sunbathing. Instead, what the swim staff had cooked up for them, in the wake of one of the most exhausting experiences of their collective lives, was swim drills.

Swim drills involved all sorts of relays of diving, paddling, treading, and—yes, that old favorite, floating, strung together in an endless stream of combinations and overseen by Landon, the head of the swim staff, who puffed on his whistle like his life depended on it.

Landon was cute, Priya thought, but that didn't excuse the whole . . . *drilling thing.*

And he really needed to cool it with his whistle.

She felt a nudge in her side and found Josie prodding her. "You're up after Jenna," Josie said, indicating that Priya should start making her way down to the edge of the water sooner rather than later.

Priya sighed. "Great, put me after Superathlete, why don't you? Make me look even better." Priya was a fine swimmer, but nothing like Jenna, who, ever since she'd kicked her fear of diving a few summers ago, rocked it out every time she got into the water.

Josie smiled. "You'll be fine. Do you have your swim tag?"

Priya nodded. "Yup, it's right—" she trailed off, realizing that, in fact, her swim tag *wasn't* "right" anywhere. It was a thin plastic tag that each camper got after taking his or her swim test that indicated which level of water he or she could swim in. It came on a stretchy cord that you could wear around your wrist so that it would be easy to take to and from the waterfront. When it was time to go in, you hung your tag on a board indicating which section of the water you were swimming in. That way, in case of any emergency, the lifeguards could tell at a glance how many swimmers were in the water, even if they weren't all in plain view.

It was a whole thing. A systemy thing.

And now there would be another whole

thing, because wouldn't you know it? Priya had forgotten hers.

"I'm sorry, Josie, I spaced," she said, grinning ruefully. "I think my brain is still mushy from all of the adventurousness of the weekend." She cocked an eyebrow hopefully. "Does that mean that I get to skip drills?"

"Nice try," Josie replied, shaking her head. "No, what that means is that you get to go back to the bunk—*quickly*—and get your swim tag. I'll just send Chelsea in after Jenna."

"Thanks a lot!" Chelsea protested from her cross-legged position on her towel. "I can't swim as well as Jenna."

"None of us can," Priya reminded her. To Josie, she said, "I'll be back as soon as I can."

▲ ▲ ▲

"*As soon as I can*," Priya decided, didn't necessarily have to mean *that* soon. In a fit of empowerment, she chose to take the scenic route back to the tent, which involved winding her own path around the rec hall on the way upslope.

Whatever, she thought. Josie wouldn't be too upset. Or, if she was, she'd get over it. Priya was still all kinds of sore from all of the hiking. The slope needed to be wound around as opposed to charged up. There was just no alternative, alas.

Once her bunk was in plain sight, she took her sweet time on her way to the front door, planning to grab her swim tag, maybe splash some water on her face, and head back out. After all, she couldn't *really* keep Josie waiting forever—no matter how much she might have wanted to.

The moment she stepped inside, though, she stopped in her tracks.

There, right before her eyes, was Joanna—with her hands deep inside Avery's trunk!

"Oh my gosh!" Priya said before she could catch herself. "Avery is going to *kill* you if she catches you snooping around!"

Joanna whipped her head toward Priya, her eyes wide and panicked. "Um, no," she stammered. "I was just, uh, borrowing her lip gloss. She said I could . . ." she trailed off, looking defeatedly back into the black hole that had once been Avery's pristinely-packed trunk. "She's going to kill me," she concluded, miserably. "There's no way I'm going to get this back to the order that I found it in."

"She's your target, huh?" Priya asked. Assassin-fever had dimmed slightly while they were all fending for themselves and fighting for their lives in the wild, but now that they were back, it was on again in full force. Either way, it was funny just to see Joanna elbow-deep in Avery's private belongings.

Or, it *would* have been funny, Priya decided, if Joanna didn't look like she was going to throw up.

Priya made a quick decision. "I won't tell," she said. Okay, fine, not the most competitive strategy, but Joanna looked like she was going to lose her mind. A little reassurance—and a promise to keep Joanna's secret safe—was literally the least she could do. "And I can help you put that back in order." She nodded toward the clothing explosion.

"Seriously?" Joanna's eyes lit up. "That would be so awesome. If I don't make it back to swim drills soon, they'll start worrying about me."

Priya crossed the floor and kneeled down next to Joanna, scooping a heap of T-shirts out of the trunk and beginning to fold them methodically.

"Honestly, though," Joanna said, lowering her voice so she suddenly sounded much more serious. "It's really nice of you to help me. I mean, I know that Avery and all the rest of our friends haven't been that nice to you Lakeview girls since you got to camp. That I haven't been that nice to you." She flushed guiltily.

"That's true," Priya admitted. "But . . . two wrongs don't make a right, I guess. And I would *really* hate to see what would happen to you if Avery came back and found her trunk looking like this. I'd be an accomplice to a very ugly crime."

Joanna giggled. Priya couldn't believe how much nicer Joanna seemed when she wasn't around Avery. And she bet that Joanna wasn't the only one stuck under Avery's thumb.

Laugh-sucking Avery had to be stopped at all costs.

"Also? I *really* detest swim drills."

Joanna burst out laughing at that. "Drills aren't so bad," she protested. "You get used to them, and, you know—eventually you get caught up in the spirit of competition and everything."

"If you insist," Priya replied. "I'm just gonna have to take your word for it."

The girls worked in silence for a few moments, giving Priya the chance to marvel at Avery's vast wardrobe. The girl had polo shirts in every color of the rainbow and then some. And the tank tops! She had tank tops of every length, weight, ribbing, texture, print, and pattern! Even if camp ran year-round, Priya thought, Avery wouldn't have a chance to wear every single article of clothing she'd brought with her for the summer.

"You know, I'm, ah, glad you showed up here, to tell you the truth," Joanna said suddenly, breaking the silence. Her expression was tentative, but she seemed resigned to charge forward with what-ever it was she was trying to say. "Not just because I needed help cleaning up. But, uh, because . . . I kinda found something."

"Avery's spoon?" Priya guessed.

"Nope." Joanna shook her head. "Better. Or maybe worse. I don't know. It's a secret, and I feel kinda weird about knowing it."

Priya finally put her folding down and turned her complete attention to Joanna. "Okay, you must spill. Now." She settled into a comfortable cross-legged position on the floor and folded her hands in her lap, like a patient child at story time.

Joanna glanced at the floor, then looked back up. "So, you know how there was this rumor that Avery used to take that one bed in every tent so that she could sneak out and meet her boyfriend?"

Priya nodded, recalling all too vividly Avery's reaction that first day when she discovered that Brynn had inadvertently taken her bed. Her ears had barely stopped ringing from the shrieks of indignation.

"But then this year, her boyfriend supposedly wasn't here?" Joanna posed this as a question.

"Well, you would know, wouldn't you? If her boyfriend was here?" Priya pointed out. "Since you're friends and all?"

"No way. She keeps that kind of stuff a secret," Joanna explained. "But we heard the same rumors that you heard—that whoever she'd been seeing was gone this year."

"But she still sneaks out of the tent at night all the time," Priya mused, starting to catch Joanna's drift. It wasn't like she and her friends had never wondered where it was that Avery disappeared to at night, though they'd long since decided that a) she was probably just visiting her friends in other tents and b) since Avery clearly didn't care about them, they couldn't be bothered to care about her. Much.

"Right. *And* . . . I just found—THESE!" Joanna reached under Avery's mattress and pulled out three manila envelopes. She lifted the flap of one to reveal a stash of envelopes. Priya squealed. She couldn't help herself. "Are those what I think they are?" Envelopes. Hand-written envelopes. This was *big*.

Joanna nodded, eyes shining. "They're *love letters*! They're not signed—I already checked," she confessed. "And she kept them, instead of giving them to whomever she's writing them to. Which, okay, is extra weird. But if you read them, you'll see that whoever these letters are for is *totally* at camp this summer! She's been writing these love letters to some guy at camp!"

"Omigosh!" Priya exclaimed, clapping a hand over her mouth in excitement. "That is the juiciest gossip ever!" She leaned closer to Joanna conspiratorially. "Who do you think it is?"

"I have *no idea*," Joanna said, shaking her head. "Trust me, I've been racking my brain."

Priya rubbed her hands together like a cartoon villain. "We need to get to the bottom of this," she proclaimed. "I propose—an alliance!"

Joanna appeared to consider this. "Like, we'll investigate together?" Her eyes sparkled with interest.

Priya nodded. "Totally. We'll go undercover and figure this out. But the one catch is that all of the Lakeview girls have to be let in on the scoop. It's too good not to be shared."

Joanna frowned. She was obviously doubtful about the wisdom of this plan.

Priya placed a reassuring hand on Joanna's arm. "I promise you—you can trust my friends. They'll be so psyched that you included them in this, they'd never rat you out. They're cool girls," she said.

Joanna looked Priya straight in the eye. "I know. I could always tell that." She wrinkled her forehead, thinking for a moment. "Yeah, I guess that would be okay. For you to tell them, I mean."

Priya grinned. "So, does this mean we're on?

Operation Mystery Love is a go?"

"Ew," Joanna shrieked, laughing. "Not if you insist on calling it that cheesetastic name."

"Whatever," Priya said, waving her hand dismissively. "We'll come up with something cooler. Nat and Sloan are good at that kind of stuff. But the name is, like, the least important part of it. The most important part is getting the dirt on who Avery's boyfriend is." She squinted mischievously at Joanna. "And if there's one thing I can promise you, it's that the Lakeview girls are geniuses when it comes to getting the gossip."

"I hope so," Joanna said, grinning. "'Cause I have a feeling that this secret is a good one!"

chapter TWELVE

Sarah was worried.

There were lots of reasons for Sarah to be worried, mainly because she'd told her Walla Walla friends . . . things. Things that were maybe, possibly, sort of the opposite of true. Things that she really wouldn't want to see revealed, uncovered, or otherwise unraveled.

She'd been worried about all of this since she'd first learned that Natalie, Jenna, and the rest of the Lakeview crew had touched down on Walla Walla territory. That much was natural. It made sense, as much as any of this whole stupid mess that she had created made sense.

And now they knew. Her secret was out. Maybe they weren't saying anything yet, but they knew. It was so obviously just a matter of time. She'd seen the looks that they'd been giving her: in the mess hall, at the waterfront, at evening activity each night. The Lakeview girls weren't going to let her lie go—it was just a question of when they were going to bring it up and throw it in her face.

As if suspicions weren't high enough with the game going on. Every nerve ending in Sarah's body felt electrified. She was petrified at what would happen when her secret finally came out to Avery and the rest of the Walla Walla girls.

So far, Natalie hadn't been tagged in Assassin. Which meant that someone, somewhere, was probably out there trying to find her spoon *at that very moment*. Possibly even Avery.

And while Natalie had—blessedly—decided to stay mum on certain details of her life since she'd arrived at camp, there was a high probability that she'd have trouble keeping things under wraps once whomever had her for a target kicked it into high gear.

So, yeah. Sarah was worried. Right about now, the only thing that she had going for her was the fact that Natalie didn't seem to want people to know who her father was any more than Sarah wanted that information out in the open. But that couldn't last forever. The truth always found a way out.

Grr. She'd been filing at the same pinky nail for at least twenty minutes now. People were bound to notice that she was acting a little weird. Edgy. She glanced around her tent. Everyone was perched on their respective bunks, engrossed in some appropriately quiet activity. So that was something. Maybe she couldn't control or keep tabs on the whole entire camp, but at least her own tent was accounted for.

She sighed, finally setting the emery board

aside. It wasn't as if she really cared about having smooth, even fingernails, anyway. She'd just wreck them during archery, softball, or the ropes course again tomorrow.

"I'll be back in ten minutes. Twenty."

Sarah looked up to find one of her tentmates, Shawn, negotiating with their counselor, Tara, for a brief reprieve from quiet hour lockdown. Sarah immediately set her nail stuff aside. "Where are you going?" she asked, wishing that her voice didn't sound quite so squeaky and awkward.

Shawn looked at her strangely. "I just have to . . . get something."

Sarah's heart leaped into her chest. What if Shawn was heading over to the Oak tent to do some Assassin recon? What if Shawn had Natalie as a target?

Even if she *didn't* have Natalie as a target, any kind of poking around could turn up some info that Sarah didn't want uncovered. "I can come with you," she offered haltingly. "I could use some fresh air."

"I thought you were *dying* after swim drills," Hailey pointed out.

Right. That. "Yeah, but I have to walk it off or I'll cramp, you know? I need to stay loose."

Good cover. Not.

"I'm, uh, just going to the rec hall for, like, a minute. It's really not worth you coming." Now Shawn was starting to sound downright irritated.

"Sure, okay. Whatever." Sarah flopped back down on her bed. She knew when she'd been outmaneuvered. Who knew what Shawn was up to? Maybe nothing. Certainly it could have been totally unrelated to Assassin, anyway. And now Sarah had just acted like a total weirdo for no good reason.

But it's not *"no good reason,"* she mused to herself, staring at the springs of the bunk above her. *It's an* excellent *reason.*

It's just not a reason that I can let anyone else in on. Ever.

▲ ▲ ▲

The counselors were off at a post-lights-out meeting again, which Natalie didn't mind one bit. She was taking the opportunity to catch up on her snail-mail exchange with Hannah. But she was struggling. She angled her flashlight in the crook of her neck so that it was aimed toward her notebook, which kept shifting in her lap. She felt as twisted as a trapeze artist, and her neck was starting to pinch.

She was just about to try and make a go of it one last time when her exercise in futility was interrupted by the sound of someone tiptoeing toward the front of the tent. It was Chelsea.

"Where are *you* going?" Nat called, teasing.

Chelsea smiled shyly. "I told Connor I'd go meet him by the big rock."

At that, all of the girls broke out into a chorus of whistles, as quietly as they could so as not to be overheard by anyone outside.

"Ew, stop it," Chelsea protested, but it was easy to see from her face that she was loving the attention. Or maybe that was just crush-glow. Either way, Natalie decided, it suited her.

"Seriously guys, give it a rest. So she's not, like, five years old like the rest of you are. Big deal," Avery said, stepping forward toward the door herself. "Some of us have lives, you know."

With that, she turned and left the tent.

"Well, I guess *Avery* has a life, then," Natalie quipped.

Chelsea flashed her friends a blank look and then followed Avery out, calling "see ya!" over her shoulder as she left.

For a moment, no one said anything. Then Priya broke the silence.

"You know what that was about, Joanna," she said. "Now's our chance!"

"Hell-o-oh!" Natalie exclaimed. "Speaking in riddles? Not helpful. If you know something, you must share!" What on earth was Priya going on about? And since when was she so chummy with Joanna?

"It's not my information to share," Priya said. "Sorry."

"Well, *whose* is it, then?" Jenna chimed in, sounding every bit as exasperated as Natalie was feeling. If there was something secret going down after hours at camp, the girls wanted to know!

"Actually, mine."

It was Joanna. Literally the *last* person in the entire world that Natalie would have expected to want to share dirt with the Lakeview girls. But Nat wasn't one to turn away a new friend. Especially not if there was a good story behind it.

"What's going on?" Natalie asked, finally rousing from bed and indicating that the rest of the girls should join her in the middle of the tent. She settled herself on the floor and looked at Joanna expectantly.

Joanna glanced at Priya, who nodded reassuringly, and then back at the group. "We have to follow her," Joanna said. "I can explain on the way."

"Ooh, drama!" Brynn squealed, hopping up and slipping her feet into her sneakers. "I'm in!"

The girls quickly got themselves together and made their way out of the tent, trying to keep their commotion to a minimum, with Priya and Joanna leading the way. After a brief survey, they realized that Avery had headed off in the direction of the waterfront.

Jenna and Brynn wanted to know all about what Joanna knew, and why they were trailing Avery. Which, of course, Natalie herself wondered, too. But just then Sloan popped up, a questioning expression on her face.

"Can I talk to you for a minute?" Sloan asked, placing a hand on Natalie's arm and looking extremely concerned.

"Sure," Natalie replied, a little bit confused.

"It's just—" Sloan bit her lip, looking conflicted about something. "Jenna and I have been talking—do you think it's weird the way that Brynn is suddenly so interested in Reed?" she blurted. "I mean, we know that he came to camp to be with you, and you guys are, like, together and stuff, and yet, she's kind of . . . always hanging all over him and stuff!" She took a deep breath. "I'm sorry. I would never think of her as the kind of girl who would go after someone else's guy. But it's weird. And we're worried about keeping the peace among the Lakeview girls. So what gives? Are you worried at all? You don't seem worried at all. So I—*we*—Jenna and I, I mean—we just don't get it."

Natalie took a moment to gather her thoughts. Then, suddenly, her mouth split into a smile and she burst out laughing.

"It's not funny," Sloan protested, miffed. "Come on." She looked extremely put out that Natalie wasn't taking this intervention seriously. Especially since it had obviously been the subject of much debate between her and Jenna.

"No, okay, sorry. It's totally not funny." Natalie straightened her arms at her side and rearranged her features into a more serious expression. After a moment, though, the corners of her mouth began to twitch again.

Her friends were looking out for her. How cute was *that*?

Sloan sighed.

"Sorry!" Natalie said again. "Look—this is me, being serious. But there's nothing to worry about. Brynn and I totally talked about it. It's just kind of a secret, is all."

At the mention of a secret, Sloan's eyes lit up. Everyone loved a good secret.

"The reason that Brynn's been stalking Reed is because . . . he's her Assassin target!"

Sloan's mouth dropped open. She looked utterly stunned.

"I mean, we didn't want everyone to know, 'cause it's a competition and stuff, but yeah—that's what's been going on." Now her eyes did turn solemn. "I'm *so* sorry that you got the wrong impression. Maybe we should have said something to you, so that you guys wouldn't have to worry about all of our friendships—"

"No," Sloan said, cutting her off. Her own mouth started to twitch at the corners, too. "I can't believe how badly Jenna and I overreacted. I hope you're not mad at us for butting into your business." She slapped her palm to her forehead. "Oh my gosh, we're such dorks. We were so worried. I can't believe it never even occurred to us that Reed would be Brynn's target." She giggled. "Okay, I'm not the most competitive person. But Jenna lives and breathes games and that kind of stuff. She should have realized. She has no excuse." She bit her lip. "So, are you mad?"

"Are you kidding?" Nat asked, laughing even harder. "I'm just lucky I have friends who are always watching my back."

"That's us," Sloan confirmed. "Back watchers. We'll keep an eye on Reed's back, too—just for Brynn's sake. *And* we won't tell anyone that he's her target."

"Good," Natalie said, patting Sloan on

the shoulder. "And I won't tell Brynn that you thought—even for a millisecond—that she was a boyfriend stealer."

They shook hands jokingly. "It's a deal," Sloan said.

Natalie laughed again. She had the best friends in the world. Nothing would ever change that. And maybe that's why she didn't have the energy to be really mad at Sarah. Because Sarah didn't have such great friends in the Walla Walla girls. And that was just . . . sad.

Sloan glanced ahead toward the rest of the group. "Wait up, guys!" she whispered as loudly as she could. She looked at Natalie. "We've gotta run."

Natalie grinned at Sloan and grabbed her hand as tightly as she could. "Let's go."

🏕 🏕 🏕

"Are you sure we're still on the right trail?" Sloan asked, flexing her leg muscles as the group made their way down the slope to the waterfront. She was still a little sore from all of the hiking they'd done over the weekend, though without a doubt, her legs were way stronger then they'd been at the beginning of the summer.

Still, ow.

"I can't see Avery at all," she whined. I can't make out her aura in this dark. And it's not like I have a divining rod or anything."

"Some of us who are less psychically gifted

rely perfectly nicely on good, old-fashioned *instinct*," Priya teased, reaching out for Joanna's shoulder to help keep her balance.

"You are referring to what's known in the New Age woo-woo community as *vibes*," Sloan countered. "And I'm sorry, but I'm just not getting any."

"Shh!" Joanna cut in. "Look—she's right there. We've got to make ourselves scarce." She looked at Sloan. "You may have vibes, but I've been going to camp with Avery for years. I have history."

"You also have a loud whisper," Priya chided. "We need to disappear. We can duck behind the swim shack," she suggested. "We'll be able to see who she's meeting."

"I can't *believe* she's had her boyfriend here all summer and managed to keep it a secret from everyone!" Sloan mused. The whole thing really blew her mind. Especially the part where Joanna was, in fact, kind of awesome. Kind of *really* awesome. She wished they'd all known this earlier. For now, they'd just have to make up for lost time. "I'm usually pretty good at picking up on that sort of stuff."

"Vibes," Priya said, nodding. They both giggled. Joanna and Priya had filled everyone in on the letters that they'd found in Avery's trunk on the way down to the waterfront, and of course the Lakeview girls were all about the latest fact-finding mission.

Natalie, Brynn, and Jenna caught up to the group and joined them in a cluster behind the swim shack. The night air was chilly against Sloan's skin, but her anticipation kept her too hopped-up to notice. She watched, breathless, as Avery crept slowly to the edge of the water, dipping a flip-flop-clad toe in, looking eager.

Even Avery could look eager and happy under the right circumstances, Sloan noted. She added that to her list of unexpected Walla Walla discoveries: Avery looking happy, peaceful, friendly.

"Someone's coming!" Jenna whispered. The girls tensed, grabbing at one another's arms eagerly.

Sure enough, someone was coming. Footsteps made soft padding noises against the sand. Avery turned, her face lighting up.

And then *Avery* ran and hid.

Whoever her boyfriend was, he wasn't in on the secret, either. Avery's crush was obviously only from afar.

Her visitor pivoted, throwing moonlight across the planes of his face. He had some friends with him, two other boys. The three of them were laughing and enjoying the cool night hair, tossing a football back and forth as they wandered closer to the edge of the water.

Sloan realized who he was at exactly the same time as the other girls did.

She could tell, because they all gasped together. (As quietly as they could.) Fortunately, Avery was too involved in her visitor to hear them.

"Oh. My. *Wow*." Natalie breathed, noiseless as a butterfly's wings.

Sloan couldn't have agreed more.

chapter

THIRTEEN

"I still can't believe it," Jenna said, squinting into the bright sunlight as it bounced off the surface of the lake.

She, Sloan, Natalie, Priya, Brynn, and Joanna were sitting in a rowboat in three rows of two, doing their best to keep the boat moving forward in a straight line while simultaneously rehashing their big-time discovery of the night before.

The identity of Avery's quote unquote boyfriend , that was.

"I know," Priya said, shaking her head as if to show just exactly how much she, like Jenna, was in disbelief at the information. "I mean, *Jackson*? He's so *old*! I think he's, like, in high school already!"

Jackson. C.I.T. Jackson of the ropes course, and Tucker's (admittedly adorable) assistant. He was funny, he was athletic, and he was definitely cute.

Unfortunately, he was a C.I.T. And way too old for Avery.

"Yup," Joanna confirmed, looking grim. "You guys, I know you're not exactly Avery's biggest fans, but this is so sad. She has a huge crush on someone who totally doesn't know she's alive. She *follows him around*, spying on him. It's . . . pathetic." She looked sorry to have to admit it.

Jenna wasn't wild about Avery, sure, but this new development had activated her pity button. Here Avery was, pretending as if she knew everything about everyone, and meanwhile, she was pining away for someone who was completely out of her league. "Pathetic" was definitely the word for it.

Jenna was sympathetic. Sort of. It wasn't like she was going to run around spreading this news or selling it to the highest bidder like tabloid fodder . . . but that being said, it wasn't like she and her friends couldn't use this information to maybe, um . . . *suggest* that Avery take a kinder, gentler tack with the Lakeview crew than she'd been doing so far. Suddenly they had leverage, in the form of a really juicy secret. Avery would *die* if she thought anyone knew she'd been sneaking around, trailing Jackson like some sort of silly schoolgirl.

The first question was whether or not to use their newfound knowledge. Then the next questions became: how, when, and, of course, the most vimportant question of all: what would they get for their troubles in the end?

Jenna kind of couldn't wait to find out.

"I can't believe we didn't realize," Natalie said, breaking into Jenna's thoughts. "I mean, she's always trying to get his attention and stuff during ropes, and when she was bugging him with the marshmallows?

On the Outdoor Adventure Weekend?"

Jenna shrugged. "Maybe we *should* have realized. But even so, we know now." She grinned mischievously. "And you know what they say: Knowledge is power."

▲ ▲ ▲

Rowing worked up an appetite, Natalie realized, as she and her tentmates made their way to the mess hall. Whatever lunch was, it was bound to be inedible, but that didn't stop her from—could it actually be?—looking *forward* to it.

I've officially been here too long, she thought to herself. *That, or I'm a victim of mind control or something like that.*

Or maybe she was just wasting away from all of the outdoor activity and stuff. Either way, she was pushing forward with the crowd through the just-opened doors as if she hadn't eaten in months.

Jenna reached their table first and waved to Natalie and the others to hurry up. Chelsea turned to Natalie, though, to explain, "I'm just gonna say hi to Connor quickly. Save me a seat."

"Will do," Natalie said, enjoying how gushy Chelsea got whenever Connor's name came up in conversation.

"Ugh, throwing yourself at a guy? Pathetic," Avery sniffed, passing by at just the right moment to spread her own personal blend of sunshine.

Natalie steeled herself against making her own nasty retort, or worse. After all, Avery was the queen of throwing herself at a guy who didn't even know she was alive, wasn't she? But Natalie also realized at the very same moment that Avery *had* to be stopped. The girl was impossible and needed a healthy dose of her own medicine.

She settled into her seat and turned to Brynn, who was sitting right next to her. "We need a plan," she announced firmly.

"I have a plan," Brynn said. "Don't you worry. I am brimming with plan."

"An Avery plan?" Natalie asked, confused, wondering when Brynn had had a chance to come up with something like that.

"A Reed plan," Brynn clarified. "A sting operation. To eliminate him from Assassin. But there's one thing—I need help. Will you do it?"

"Be your partner in crime as you plot to take down my boyfriend?" Natalie asked. Brynn nodded, and she smiled.

"Of course," she replied. "Count me in."

Plans were good. Natalie was way into plans. And thank goodness, her friends were, too.

So far, Brynn's plan was working like a charm.

Not that she was surprised, of course— she'd thought it through and it was a solid plan. Very . . . planny, just waiting to be executed by two masterminds like Natalie and herself.

When she and Natalie first got down to the waterfront for instructional swim, she'd complained of stomach cramps. As the campers all broke off into their swim groups, she lurched forward and grabbed at her stomach, moaning dramatically.

"What is it, Brynn?" Landon asked, hovering over her, concerned.

"I don't know . . . ohh." She had stayed doubled over since that had seemed to be having its desired effect on Landon. "I think . . . maybe I accidentally ate something I shouldn't have at lunch. Like, maybe I'm having an allergy or something."

"Your counselors should have a list of all of the food allergies in their tent," Landon had pointed out, not unkindly.

"Um, maybe it's, like, an allergy that *I didn't even know I had*." She had groaned again for good measure.

"Or maybe she's lactose intolerant," Natalie had said, stepping forward with authority. "Like, my mom can eat a little bit of goat cheese on her salad but not, you know, a whole thing of fro-yo or anything like that, and we did have that pasta with the cheese sauce for lunch so maybe it was, like, just too much for her or something."

Brynn had been impressed with Nat's improv skills. Maybe her father was right—maybe she did have the acting gene buried somewhere inside there. But that was a conversation for another day, when they didn't have plans and other important stuff in the works.

"I'll take her to the nurse, just to be safe," Natalie had offered. "If she's this uncomfortable, someone should go with her, don't you think?" then she'd broken out her most wide-eyed, innocent expression.

It hadn't been completely clear from the look on his face—mainly because from her position, Brynn hadn't been able to *see* Landon's face, or really any part of him other than his bare, tanned feet—how he felt about this plan, but Natalie hadn't given him any time to nix it. Instead, she'd grabbed Brynn by the shoulders and gently led her up and toward the path away from the waterfront.

It had all happened too quickly for Landon to offer much protest.

Now the two girls stood poised in the center of Reed's tent.

"Are you ready for this?" Brynn, who had made a miraculous recovery, grinned at Natalie.

Natalie nodded. "I'll take his cubby. You go under the bed?"

"Perfect," Brynn said.

They got to work.

Brynn was finding all sorts of things—a stray gym sock (gross), a music magazine, a package of double-stuff Oreos—but nothing that was remotely spoonlike.

And then she hit the mother lode.

"*What* is this?" she shrieked.

"Brynn, you gave me a heart attack," Natalie chided. "What did you find under there, a shrunken head?"

"Scarier than that," Brynn said, beckoning Nat over. "Look." She slid out the offending object and plunked it down on the bed accusatorily.

Natalie's eyes grew wide. "Is that what I think it is?"

Brynn nodded in terror. "A *home. Waxing. Kit.*" She shuddered. "Do you think . . . he waxes his chest?" Brynn asked. She had read that sometimes athletes did that, like wrestlers or swimmers, when they wanted to make themselves more sleek or aerodynamic.

Of course, as far as she knew, Reed was neither a wrestler nor a swimmer. She couldn't imagine why he would need to be sleek or aerodynamic.

A terrible thought occurred to her. "Or—oh, no—what if he waxes . . ." she paused for effect ". . . his *eyebrows?*"

Natalie and Brynn both shuddered, and then burst into hysterics. The thought was too awful to contemplate.

"I can't think about that," Natalie said. "Because if I do, I will be forced to confront the fact that my boyfriend might have better manicured eyebrows than I do. And that is upsetting."

Brynn was laughing so hard that she wiped a tear from the edge of her eye. "Did you find anything in the cubbies?"

Natalie cracked up all over again. "Yeah, but I wasn't going to say anything because it was too embarrassing."

Brynn merely pointed to the waxing kit by way of response. How could *anything* be more embarrassing than that?

"He has an emery board and a nail buffer," Natalie said, the words coming out in a guilty rush.

"And a special Italian hair gel that I happen to know you can only get online. And, uh, the worst thing of all—a *nose hair* trimmer!" She looked truly traumatized by this final revelation.

"Oh, Natalie," Brynn said, shaking her head wearily and feeling genuinely sorry for her friend. No one wanted to have to think about their guy's nose hairs.

"He *was* being kinda . . . prissy on the camping trip," Natalie said, "and it weirded me out a little. But I decided I was being unfair, since *I* was being kinda prissy on the camping trip, too. But this . . ." Natalie swept her arm out, as though to indicate all of the swanky toiletries that they had uncovered. "I don't—" she stopped abruptly as the two of them both realized that they heard a voice outside. "Is that—" Natalie asked.

"Reed," Brynn finished, recognizing the voice. "Outside. Now." Instantly, she mobilized. "Okay, you stay in here and organize things as best as you can. I'll go stall him. I'll try and get him away from the tent. Once you hear our voices fade, you sneak out."

Natalie saluted her. "Got it. You're such the little international woman of mystery."

Brynn winked at Natalie over her shoulder. "Don't you forget it."

Outside, she found a very surprised-looking Reed about to walk into his tent.

"*There* you are!" she exclaimed, all enthusiasm and energy. Meanwhile, she beamed psychic energy at him. *Don't go inside. Don't go inside. Don't go inside.*

It actually looked like it might be working. *Score one for Sloan and all of her crazy woo-woo ideas*, Brynn thought. "Omigosh! I've been looking everywhere for you."

"You have?" Was it Brynn's imagination, or did Reed actually seem kind of happy to hear that?

Huh. Weird. Almost as weird as his home waxing kit.

"Yeah, I, uh, wanted to talk to you, if you have, like, a minute."

"Definitely," Reed said, beaming. It wasn't her imagination: he was really into whatever he thought she wanted to talk about. Hmm. That was weird. "'Cause I really wanted to talk to you, too."

Now it was Brynn's turn to be confused. "About what?"

"About *this*," he said. At her blank look, he continued, "About the fact that every time I turn around these days, you're there. It's like you're following me or something."

Uh-oh. Reed was totally on to her! No way she'd win Assassin now.

Reed smiled at her slyly.

"Reed, I'm sorry," Brynn babbled.

"Brynn, don't be," Reed said. "I think it's cool that you like me."

"You think it's cool that—wait a minute. You think I *like* you?" Her jaw nearly hit the ground, she was so shocked.

"Yeah. And it's cool," Reed repeated. "I mean, *you're* cool."

"But . . . you're with Natalie," Brynn pointed out.

"But you're into me," Reed replied, as if it were the most logical thing in the world. As if just by liking him, she had the power to undo her friend's relationship.

Ew. Ew. Ew.

"But . . . you're into Natalie," Brynn repeated, thinking that if she just said it enough times, Reed would get on board and realize why this was all so problematic.

Sadly, that didn't look like it was going to be the case.

All at once, it looked like the nose hair trimmer wasn't the grossest thing about Reed anymore.

"Forget it, Brynn," Natalie said, stepping out of the tent from behind Brynn and startling her all over again. "It doesn't matter *who* Reed is into, since he obviously can't be trusted."

Brynn felt awful. She'd never meant to get her friend into a mess like this. *Then again*, she thought, *at least now Natalie knows the truth about her guy. Ick. If it were me and my dude was sort of sleazy, I'd want to know. Maybe Natalie will be happy about this.*

One glance at Natalie's face told Brynn that no way was she happy about this. To Reed, Natalie said, "I was having my doubts about you when you couldn't stop complaining about camp. I mean, I know I can be a prima donna, but it's not like I don't know how to enjoy myself." Her eyes narrowed. "I had no idea that you were so gross that you'd be into one of my friends if they showed the least little bit of interest in you."

Reed's face had turned the color of a tomato, but he was speechless. Then again, what could he possibly have said, Brynn reasoned?

"We're breaking up, Reed," Natalie said, her eyes flashing with anger now. "Oh, and one more thing—Brynn didn't *like* you, she had you as a target for Assassin. I was confused about that myself for a little bit. But apparently Brynn has better taste than I do. So you're going to give her your spoon and tell her who your target is."

"Why should I have to forfeit the game?" Reed asked, indignant.

"Because if you don't, we're going to let everyone in camp in on your own personal spa that you've got going on in there. And somehow, I doubt that you want the rest of you tent to know how you stay so pretty."

Now it was Reed's turn to let his jaw hit the ground. His face turned white, and he looked like he wanted to throw up. He closed his mouth, opened it, and then closed it again without saying anything.

Then he ran off.

Brynn whirled around to face Natalie. "Nat, I'm sorry about that—" she said.

Natalie came down the stairs so that she and Brynn were side by side. "I'm not. Gosh, he turned out to be totally uncool, huh?"

"Well, but, I can see why you liked him," Brynn said. "I mean, you didn't know—"

"Two words, Brynn: Nose hairs." Natalie

pressed her lips together in a grim line, which set the girls laughing all over again.

Brynn was glad that her friend understood the deal: Boys could be fun, but they didn't always work out. And sometimes they did icky things like tweeze their eyebrows and crush on your friends.

Girlfriends, though? Girlfriends were forever.

chapter

FOURTEEN

Sloan was halfway toward her first bite of turkey "meatloaf" (she didn't know why there were quotation marks around the word "meatloaf" on the chalkboard menu that stood outside the mess hall, and frankly, she didn't want to know) when Dr. Steve strode in and, with one short blast of the whistle that hung around his neck, commanded the attention of the entire room.

Sloan placed her fork back down on the table. "Saved by the bell," she murmured under her breath to no one in particular.

"I have an announcement to make, everyone," he began. "Because you were all such great, active participants in the Outdoor Adventure Weekend, we're going to have a special treat tomorrow night: movie night!"

Sloan's heart quickened at that news. A movie! That was almost twentieth century living, right there. Walla Walla was embracing the techno-lifestyle. Good times. She—and all of her tentmates—were sure ready for it.

And from the sounds of the cheering from everyone else in the room, so were the rest of the campers.

"Settle down," Dr. Steve said, the expression on his face showing how happy he was to be the bearer of good news. "That's not all."

The room went quiet again. *Not all?* Sloan wondered. What else could there be? Personal e-mail access for the day? GPS installed in all of the kayaks? Bluetooth pieces for them to use to call their parents?

Real meatloaf that didn't require identifying quotation marks? Or—dare she even dream it?—a pizza delivery from the outside world?

Not likely.

"The movie itself will be a surprise—but it's a surprise that I know you'll like!" And with that, Dr. Steve strode happily—and confidently—toward the kitchen, no doubt in search of something more palatable than "meatloaf."

"What do you think it's going to be?" Brynn asked, drumming her fingers enthusiastically against the tabletop. "A blockbuster? A romantic comedy? Oh, wait—maybe it'll be 3-D. Or, you know, like an IMAX or something."

"Silly, they can only screen Imax on special screens with fancy Imax equipment and stuff," Natalie reminded her. "But who cares? Whatever it is, it'll be a fun change from the whole boot camp thing we've had going on here."

Sloan laughed. "You're telling me."

"I am not exactly sure how this is considered, um, challenging," Priya said, glancing doubtfully at the taut rope that ran about twelve inches off the ground, secured in place by twin pegs on either side.

"Just try it, Priya," Tucker replied. "If you can make it from one end to the other without losing your balance, you win."

"What do I win?" Priya called out, stepping foot cautiously onto the rope. "What if the prize isn't worth it?"

The "tightrope" didn't look scary, especially not when compared to the high course that they'd conquered weeks ago. According to Tucker, in many ways the lower ropes were actually way more challenging, since they relied on balance rather than strength. That was why he warmed them up on the higher course—once they'd been way up there, they were game for almost anything else he wanted to throw at them.

Priya faltered and stumbled backward. Darn. Now she'd have to start again. Tucker was timing them to see who could get all the way across the fastest.

"It's worth it. You'll see," Tucker called.

"Go, Priya! You can do it!" Jenna called from the sidelines. Jenna had scampered sideways across the thing like she had Velcro stuck to the bottom of her shoes. She was looking like the one to beat. As usual.

"Although, actually, I have to admit—I forgot to pick up the prize!" Tucker said, realization dawning across his face. "Oops. Jackson—do you want to go get the . . . stuff?"

Jackson looked up from where he'd been winding some ropes and stacking orange pylons. "Uh, sure," he said easily. "Except . . . I think it'll take more than just me. To carry everything, I mean. Do you want me to bring someone?"

Avery jumped forward. "I'll go!" she said eagerly. Then, taking a moment to compose herself, she smoothed her hair out of her eyes and added casually, "I mean, since I've already done this and stuff."

"Sure, no problem," Tucker said, not looking up from his stopwatch. "Priya, keep it up—or no prize for you!"

But Priya could hardly be concerned with something as trivial as what prize Tucker might have had in store for her or for the rest of the tent. She was *waaay* too interested in watching Avery and Jackson jog off together. Avery was trotting off like a dog after a chew toy. For his part, Jackson had barely slowed his stride for her. Priya wondered whether anyone else had picked up on this development.

She glanced up and caught Joanna's eye. The look on Joanna's face said it all. *Of course* she had picked up on Avery rushing after Jackson. How could she possibly have missed it?

The next time Priya tripped, she slid forward off the rope, rather than backward. She was too focused to keep her mind on the course. But when Tucker ordered her back to the start of the course again, she found she didn't really mind one bit that she was losing. Not when there were so many other exciting things afoot at camp to get involved in . . .

▲ ▲ ▲

The last thing that Natalie wanted was a make-your-own sundae bar for evening activity. Not that she had anything against ice cream—far from it, she was a firm believer in the healing powers of rocky road. But Tucker's "prize" at the ropes course that afternoon had been to give all of the girls ice cream sandwiches—not just the winner, who had, of course, been Jenna—and at this point, Natalie thought she might be in danger of actually turning into a giant scoop of ice cream herself.

She was idling by the long sundae bar table, trying to avoid getting jostled by her campmates, most of whom did not share her apathy toward ice-creamy goodness, when Ian, Reed's counselor, wandered over to her.

"Hey, Natalie," he said, smiling. His hair was thick and wheat-colored, and stuck up from his head like a crew cut that was trying to grow itself out through sheer willpower, but losing the battle against the realities of science and the human body. "I have . . ." he fumbled, reaching into his back jeans pocket, fishing something out and thrusting it at her, "a letter for you. From Reed."

Natalie squinted at the proffered envelope,

then took it from him. "Reed wrote me a letter? Why would Reed write me a letter?" It occurred to her as she asked the question that she hadn't seen him at dinner that night, and he wasn't at the sundae bar, either. Hmm.

"I think he assumed you might have some questions . . . once you realized that he had gone back to L.A.," Ian said. "This was his way of saying good-bye."

Natalie was stunned. She knew that Reed had been unhappy at Walla Walla—of course she knew, you couldn't have a single conversation with Reed and not know—but she hadn't known that it was so bad that he wouldn't be able to last the summer. Suddenly she felt bad about giving him a hard time for being so prissy. Then she remembered how he had gotten all flirty with Brynn, and stopped feeling bad just as quickly as she'd started.

"Ah," she said, trying to sort out the mixture of feelings that she was experiencing.

"Walla Walla isn't for everyone," Ian said tactfully.

Natalie nodded. Inside, though, she couldn't help but think that Walla Walla may not have been for everyone, but she, at least, was not a quitter. That was for sure. Knowing that she'd been able to pull off something that other people—boy people, even— didn't have the strength for made her feel totally proud of herself and excited about how the summer was shaking out. Okay, so Walla Walla wasn't at all what she had expected when she signed up, but she was making the best of it. And doing a darn good job of that, as well.

"I hope the letter answers some of your questions," Ian said and went off, presumably to locate some of his own campers, or maybe even to pig out on ice cream.

Once Ian had left, Natalie ripped open the envelope and scanned her letter. In it, Reed confirmed exactly what Natalie had suspected—he was not cut out for Walla Walla, but after the way that things had gone down with the two of them the other day, he was too embarrassed to tell her about his plan to leave to her face. Hence, the letter.

Dear Natalie,

By now you must know that I'm on my way back to L.A. I hope you don't think I'm too lame for leaving, but Outdoor CORE was just too much for me to take.

Even with all of the Outdoor Adventure stuff, I still had a great time with you—you were definitely the best thing about Walla Walla.

    I hope you have a good rest of the summer (watch out for spiders in the outhouse!), and I hope you forgive me for not being able to say good-bye to your face. I miss you! Maybe we'll see each other again in L.A.

    I know you're probably upset about how I was flirting with Brynn, and I don't blame you. I really have no excuse, except to say just that I'm sorry and you deserved better than that. I hope that we can still be friends.

    —Reed

It was a little bit cowardly.

Well, no—it was a *lot* bit cowardly. But Nat still had to give a guy credit for trying to do the right thing. Even if it was sort of too little, too late.

Way too little, too late.

"Whatcha got?" Brynn asked, sidling up to Natalie and glancing over her shoulder at the letter.

"Reed. He left this for me. When he went back to L.A." Natalie looked at Brynn. "He's gone. Can you believe it?"

Brynn scanned Natalie's face. "Well, at least we know he kept up his beauty regiment while he was here. So he can hold his head high when he steps off that plane," she cracked. "But, wait—are you okay with this?" she asked, her tone serious.

Natalie was grateful that she had good friends like Brynn, people who truly cared about her feelings.

"Definitely," Nat said. And she truly meant it. How could she not be okay with Reed's departure? So what if she didn't have a boyfriend anymore. What she did have—girl power—was way better than some dumb guy who clearly couldn't be counted on.

A dumb guy who couldn't be counted on who trimmed his nose hairs. "It's better for him. He wasn't happy, you know? I think at the end of the day, he really wanted to spend the summer back in glamorous Hollywood."

Sarah knew she was in trouble the moment she heard Natalie mention the word "Hollywood." Of course, Avery, who'd been feverishly making her way through a pile of whipped cream and sprinkles (just whipped cream and sprinkles, no ice cream—it was kind of weird) had picked up on it. Her hearing was better than bat sonar. Avery immediately grabbed Sarah's elbow and dragged her over to the other end of the table, where Natalie and Brynn were discussing Reed's disappearance.

Sarah felt awful. She didn't know what had gone down between Reed and Natalie, but the last thing that she wanted to do was stir up even more trouble right in the middle of some preexisting drama. But drama, of course, was all Avery ever wanted. And Avery usually got what she wanted.

She just wasn't sure how and when *she'd* ended up one of Avery's top partners in crime.

"Too bad Reed didn't want to stick around and spend the summer with you," Avery snapped at Natalie. "But it's probably for the best. You're not exactly his type."

Natalie arched an eyebrow as Sarah cringed inwardly. "Meaning?"

"Meaning he needs someone who understands his Hollywood lifestyle," Avery said.

By now Sarah was long past the point of cringing. By now, all she wanted was a turbo-eject button that would launch her out of the rec hall and this horrible conversation for good. But this was camp, not a science fiction movie, and therefore, she was stuck right where she was.

Avery turned to Sarah.

Don't say it. Don't say it. Don't say it. Sarah tried to project her thoughts at Avery, to no avail.

"It's too bad, Sarah, that Reed didn't spend more time with you," Avery said, smirking. "Maybe then he would have found someone who, you know, *got* him. And the whole L.A. connection thing."

Sarah's face was so hot that she thought it might burst into flames. She couldn't look up, couldn't risk eye contact with Natalie or Brynn. She could feel their gazes burning a hole in her, could feel them willing her to jump in, to explain this all away. But it was too late for that. Way too late. She didn't know what to say. There wasn't anything to say. There wasn't anything to *do*.

So Sarah did nothing. Said nothing. And when Avery stalked away from the Lakeview girls, Sarah followed mutely at her heels.

chapter
FIFTEEN

Something was different, Chelsea realized.

It was the morning after the ice cream sundae bar, and even though no one looked especially excited to be trudging upslope to calisthenics, there was a buzz, an energy in the air that was totally impossible to ignore.

Luckily, her friend Jenna wasn't the type to ignore it.

After doing some fact-finding, Jenna slipped subtly into formation next to Chelsea and immediately launched into her stretches and toe-touches.

"Well?" Chelsea whispered impatiently.

"It's Assassin. It's almost over," Jenna explained. "Last night at the sundae bar, MaryEllen Masters called Heather Duffy out for bringing her spoon to the social and *eating with it!*"

Eating ice cream with your spoon. Huh. It was actually a vaguely genius plan, Chelsea realized. Except, of course, for how it had backfired.

So not so genius after all. She chuckled to herself.

"So how many people are left?" Chelsea asked.

"Just a few. But according to some of the older campers, the game won't last much more than the night. Once it gets down to this few people, someone makes a mistake and leaves their spoon someplace obvious or out in the open. Everyone's all sloppy and tired."

Chelsea found that she actually felt sort of let down by this news. Sure, she'd been out of the game for a while now, but she had still been somewhat swept up in Assassin-fever. For all that Avery was a pain in the butt, the suggestion about the game had been a smart one. It had really brought everyone together, even the Lakeview girls.

"I'm bummed," Jenna said, echoing Chelsea's thoughts. "I mean, even though I've been captured and everything, it was still kind of neat knowing that the game was going on, and people were being all weird and twitchy and stuff. And, you know, it kind of gave us all permission to snoop around in one another's things and be sneaky."

"Always fun," Chelsea agreed. She definitely wasn't above being sneaky now and then.

Inside, though, she had to wonder: Was the end of the game really such a bad thing, after all? Some of them had uncovered some not-fabulous things about their so-called friends, hadn't they? Natalie sure had, when it came to Reed. And if there were any other skeletons tucked away in any closets, Chelsea wondered if they might not be better off staying buried at this point. She didn't know what would happen if the other girls—the Walla Walla girls—figured out that Sarah had lied to them about who her father was. That was bound to lead to fireworks—the bad kind of fireworks. And the last thing any of them needed was fireworks.

Hadn't there already been enough trouble this summer? She sure thought so.

▲ ▲ ▲

Natalie sighed. Archery was so not her thing.

Not to mention, it was *hard*. The strings on her bow were set so tightly that her arms had to strain against the tension. She was grunting with exertion and wiping beads of sweat off of her upper lip. All in all, it was not her most glamorous moment.

"Sarah!" Natalie looked up to see that Jonathan, the archery instructor, was beckoning Sarah toward Natalie, who stood at the ready, bow poised. Not surprising, since Sarah was a natural at archery.

"Sarah," Jonathan called, "can you work with Natalie on her stance, please? I've got to set up the targets for next period."

The deer-in-the-headlights look on Sarah's face mirrored Natalie's own internal panic, but she tried not to let it show. She willed herself to be as calm and normal as possible as Sarah ambled over, clearly stiff and uncomfortable.

"Uh, I think the problem is that you've got your feet too close together," Sarah ventured, glancing downward. "They should be farther apart, and the back leg should be straighter—" she stepped around and pressed against the back of Natalie's knee, gently forcing the leg to lock in place.

"Kind of like a reverse warrior!" Natalie exclaimed, starting to feel like she was maybe getting it.

Sarah looked at her blankly.

"In yoga," Natalie explained.

"Oh." Sarah didn't have much more to say to that.

Sarah watched, awkward and silent, as Natalie fumbled with her bow. Finally, it was too much for Natalie to bear. She put her bow down and turned to Sarah. "I just—I wanted to say to you," she began, hesitant, "that it's okay. I mean, about what you told everyone. Like, I know that you told them that your dad was a movie star, like mine is. So that people think that my life is basically yours. I'm not mad or anything."

Sarah was quiet.

"I guess I can kind of understand why you might have done it, if you were new, and feeling shy and stuff," Natalie went on, "but don't you think that if you need to lie to impress people about who you are, then maybe those people aren't really your friends after all?" She turned to look Sarah directly in the eye, but Sarah wouldn't meet her gaze.

For a moment, no one said anything. Then Sarah took a deep breath.

"How's the stance coming?" Jonathan called,

looking over to see what the girls were doing.

Quickly, Natalie scampered into place the way that Sarah had shown her. Jonathan flashed them both a thumbs-up. Natalie smiled at Sarah, hoping that maybe she'd come out with whatever had been on the tip of her tongue. But one look at Sarah confirmed that the moment was over. She'd shut down, and definitely wasn't interested in talking anymore.

Natalie couldn't believe it. She'd been so understanding, giving Sarah the perfect opening. And still, it wasn't enough. Sarah wasn't going to talk.

So that was that, Natalie realized. At least for the foreseeable future.

"Sorry that archery turned out to be kind of a bummer for you," Jenna said, patting Natalie on the shoulder consolingly. "You have other skills and talents. That's why we love you."

"Gee, you're sweet," Natalie said, pushing a chicken finger across her plate without enthusiasm. "And here I thought my sole purpose in life was to win the world over with my athletic skills."

The girls were chowing down after a long day, despite the fact that the dinner option left more than a little bit to be desired. The good news was that tonight was the much-anticipated movie night! Even Jenna, who knew that she was enjoying her time at Walla Walla more than some of her fellow Lakeview girls were, was looking forward to some real-world relaxation. "We're gonna have fun tonight," she assured Natalie. "No more thinking about horrible things like sports. What do you think the movie is going to be?"

Natalie shrugged. "That's the thing about a surprise. I expect to be surprised. I literally have no idea." She stuck her tongue out at Jenna.

"Ha-ha." Jenna munched on a carrot stick thoughtfully. "I wonder if it's going to be something with, like, a summer theme or something. You know? Anyway, David said he and the guys were going to head over to the rec room early to save seats. So we can sit with them if we want."

"Cool," Natalie said. "It's nice that you guys are good with being friends even though the boyfriend-girlfriend thing didn't work out."

"Right?" Jenna agreed. "I think we're just better this way. But what about you? I'm just sorry that Reed turned out to be kind of lame in the end."

Natalie opened her mouth to reply, but before she could, Avery jumped in. "Please. That's what you get for going for guys your own age," she said snidely. "Boys can be so immature. That's why you have to go for someone older." She gave them a withering look and returned to picking at her dinner.

Jenna wanted more than anything to jump up on the top of the table and announce to the whole entire camp that Avery had been making a fool of herself chasing after a C.I.T that she had no chance with whatsoever. All of her talk about older guys was just that—talk. She would have done it, too, if it hadn't been for Natalie shooting her a warning look.

Jenna took a deep breath and counted to ten in her head. Exposing Avery wouldn't do any good, she knew. Natalie was right. The best thing they could do was just ignore her. What was it that Sloan was always saying, anyway? Oh, yeah—it was that karma had a way of coming back to get you when you least expected it. Which meant that something was probably in store for Avery, and sooner rather than later.

Karma was a boomerang that way.

Jenna couldn't help herself. Avery hadn't made any friends of the Lakeview girls. She was just hoping that Avery got her payback. She sure did deserve it.

Sarah couldn't believe it.

No—seriously. She *couldn't. Believe. It.*

She glanced down at the spoon wrapped tightly in her fingers. It was Alton's spoon, a guy from the Redwood tent, and she'd found it in a pair of old high-topped sneakers that he'd hung from a power line that ran the length of the upslope area. In the right shoe, to be precise. And the only reason that Sarah had even known to look there was because she'd spent days watching Alton walking to and from his tent after activities and meals, and each time, he glanced at the sneakers on his way past. Until finally, she grew suspicious.

It wasn't easy. She'd had to pull a chair out under the sneakers and locate a stick that was long enough to prod the sneakers from around the wire—smacking herself in the forehead with the shoes in the process, thank you very much, and nearly falling backward off the chair and breaking her neck. But it was worth it. Anything for the game.

She'd *won*. She was tripping. This was her first year that she'd won Assassin, and she knew that Avery would be psyched (if a little bit jealous, which, Sarah had to admit, was kind of fun to imagine).

Not only that, but she'd manage to keep everything together. Under control. Maybe the Lakeview girls had discovered her horrible secret, but the Walla Walla girls hadn't.

In fact, the main reason she'd won the game at all was because her own secrets had forced her to stay constantly vigilant and on her toes.

In the end, it had all worked out. Her secrets were still safe.

Sure, okay, fine, maybe things were beyond weird with the Lakeview girls. And it was starting to look unlikely that she and Natalie would ever really be friends again. But those were just the sacrifices that she was going to have to make in order to keep her social standing with Avery and the Walla Walla crew.

Her secrets were still safe. And really, that was all that mattered, wasn't it?

Sarah felt a twinge of guilt and brushed it aside. She glanced at the bright, neon-orange face of her digital sports watch and realized that movie night was starting any second. She had to get to the rec hall. She couldn't wait to burst in and show everyone the very last spoon. She couldn't wait to announce that she had won.

She literally couldn't wait one more second. She flexed her toes, bounced on her heels, and dashed off in the direction of the rec hall to announce her stunning victory.

People were going to go *nuts* when they found out.

▲ ▲ ▲

As she drew closer to the rec hall, Sarah could hear the sounds of voices inside, chatter, laughter, and general excitement. Movie night had begun! She was late! She was missing all of the fun!

She quickened her pace, trying to calm her breathing as she made her way to the back door. With any luck, she could slip in without anyone noticing. She'd just have to announce her grand victory later on. The thought made her giddy. Would she be able to contain herself throughout the whole movie? She wasn't sure.

She pulled the door open and stepped inside.

Unfortunately, as she entered the rec hall, she didn't realize that rows of folding chairs had been set up in preparation for the movie. Sarah stomped directly into a chair, sending it crashing loudly down the aisle.

The entire room turned to gape at her.

It was only then that Sarah realized what was going on at the front of the room. Or, more specifically, *who* was at the front of the room.

Tad Maxwell. *The* Tad Maxwell, Hollywood star. Natalie's father.

Or, if you listened to what Sarah had told everyone, *Sarah's* father.

One look at everyone's faces told her that her secret was out. Way out. Completely and totally out.

Avery jumped up out of her seat, eyes flashing. "Hey, Sarah!" she called, her voice dripping with menace and anger. "Look at the *surprise* we have for movie night! *Natalie's* father, Tad Maxwell, is letting us screen his new movie before anyone else in the world sees it, as a reward for making it through the Outdoor Adventure Weekend."

Sarah's face went pale. She wanted to faint, to disappear, to launch into outer space. Anything other than to have to look at the faces of all of her disappointed, angry friends.

Make that ex-friends, she corrected herself.

"It's *Natalie's* father," Avery repeated. "Here! As a surprise! Isn't that *crazy*?"

Sarah's eyes went blurry with tears. In the distance, she could see Natalie looking at her. Natalie didn't seem angry—only worried and sympathetic.

Someone who really cared about me, Sarah thought, *and what did I do? I stole her life story. I totally used her. And then I blew her off all summer long.*

Some friend I am.

The room was so quiet you could hear a pin drop. But Sarah's heart thumped in her chest so loudly she couldn't believe no one else was hearing it. She didn't know what to do, what to say, where to go.

She dropped her spoon, her precious spoon, that only seconds ago had seemed like the most important thing in the world, on the ground. Even though it was tiny, it echoed loudly in the room.

Everyone was staring at her. Gaping. Incredulous. There was no way around this hole that she'd dug herself into. So she did the only thing she could think of to do.

She ran.

chapter

SIXTEEN

"So, what did your dad say about the whole thing?" Jenna asked Natalie. The two were making their way back to the tent for morning cleanup after breakfast and rehashing last night's major scene.

"Oh, he didn't really pick up on all of Avery's drama," Natalie said. "I just told him that she was kind of a weirdo."

What can I say? Natalie thought. *It's the truth.* She wasn't sorry. Avery had said much worse things about her and her friends, after all.

"I mean, I haven't seen him in so long, so we just wanted to hang out and talk and do some catching up. He wanted all of the gory details on the Outdoor Adventure Weekend."

"I hope you didn't hold back. You could probably win some good sympathy points, you know?" Jenna said.

Natalie smiled. "Please. We got to see his new movie first, before anyone else in the world. I don't need any more sympathy points. *The Amazon Files,* so cool. And they filmed it in the actual Amazon! But anyway, it didn't work."

"What didn't work?" Jenna asked.

"Hanging out with my dad. I mean, it worked, like, it was great to see him—and really great to go to that diner nearby and eat something not cooked by the kitchen staff—but I couldn't get my mind off of Sarah. She must have been so embarrassed last night. Even though what she did was wrong, and even though she's been so lousy to us . . . I just feel horrible for her." Natalie couldn't shake the image of Sarah's pale, scared face from the night before. It didn't matter that Sarah had lied and avoided the Lakeview girls all summer. Right now, Natalie just felt for her. Call her a sucker; she just couldn't help herself.

Jenna nodded. "I do, too. Maybe we should try to talk to her?"

Natalie stopped walking, and pointed in the near distance. She'd just spotted Sarah on her way back to her own tent. Maybe Sarah didn't deserve their sympathy or their support, but Natalie couldn't just walk away from her former friend. "Now's as good a time as any."

▲ ▲ ▲

Jenna trotted up to Sarah and called her name. "Sarah!" she said. "Hey—wait up. We want to talk to you."

Sarah stopped in her tracks, peering up at the girls. Her eyes were puffy and red-rimmed, as though she'd been crying. "No one wants to talk to me," Sarah replied sadly. "Why should you guys be any different? Or were you just going to tell me off, too?"

"We're not going to tell you off," Jenna assured her.

"Why do they want to talk to you? Because they're losers, just like you," Avery said, swooping in like a vulture, her eyes glittery and mean. "You *should* talk to them, Sarah. In fact, you should be their BFF. You guys are all such weirdos. You deserve one another."

Jenna bristled. Enough was enough. Hadn't Sarah learned her lesson by now? Hadn't they all? There was no reason to be nasty; there never had been.

She made a decision. Avery needed to be shut down. Immediately.

She stepped forward. "Maybe you're right, Avery. Maybe we do deserve one another." She put her hands on her hips and looked Avery squarely in the eye. "But that's nothing compared to what you deserve."

"Whatever," Avery snapped.

"*Whatever* is right," Jenna said. "You're not worth it to me—or to any of us. But I promise you that you're going to back off and leave Sarah—and the rest of us—alone."

Avery snorted. "Why would I do that?"

Jenna smiled sweetly. "Because if you don't, we'll tell everyone about your pathetic little crush on Jackson, and how he doesn't even know you're alive." She narrowed her eyes. "We've seen all of those love letters you wrote to him. The ones you keep under your bed. We know that you follow him around like a puppy dog. And that he couldn't care less."

Avery gasped, the color draining from her face. Obviously she had no idea her actions were so transparent. Though Jenna couldn't imagine how that could be the case. Really—she'd pelted Jackson with marshmallows. What was that, if not a declaration of unrequited crushage?

"Don't worry, we won't say anything," Jenna said. "That is, *if*, like I say, you leave us—*all* of us— alone. For the rest of the summer."

Avery squinted, then bit her lip, finally managing to choke out a response. "Fine!" she stammered. "Fine."

She raced off.

Jenna turned to Natalie and the two dissolved into giggles. Who knew the wicked witch of Walla Walla would be that easy to fell? If only they'd tried standing up to Avery sooner, maybe the summer would have gone differently.

Maybe things would have been different with Sarah.

Jenna turned to Sarah, wondering what she thought of the scene that had just played out. Maybe she'd understand that since the Lakeview girls were standing up for her, they forgave her. They wanted their old Sarah back. They wanted to try and make things work again.

But Sarah, too, had disappeared.

As much as she wasn't wild about the whole

Outdoor CORE theory, Natalie had to admit that sometimes it made a little bit of sense. Tonight, for example.

When word got around among the staff that Sarah had been making up strange stories about her past, to the disbelief of her fellow campers, they had collectively decided to organize a bunch of team-building exercises for evening activity to help restore everyone's sense of faith and camaraderie.

The Oak girls were doing trust falls. Natalie was pleased to see that Avery had adopted an entirely new persona for this exercise, one that was extremely cooperative and friendly. In fact, her whole demeanor had changed since Jenna had called her out on her crush on Jackson. Just like everyone else—Avery had things that she wanted kept close to the vest.

Of course, her new attitude was probably fake, Natalie reasoned, but it was way more pleasant to deal with than Sourpuss Avery. She'd take it. It was probably the best they were going to do this summer.

"Earth to Natalie! Are you paying attention?" It was Brynn, standing atop a short footstool, ready to fall backward into her tentmates' interlocked arms. "For this to work, we need to have *trust*." She winked. "Trust fall, you know?"

"No, I know," Natalie said, feeling distracted. "I just . . ." she caught Sarah's figure out of the corner of her eye, sitting under a tree, separate from the rest of her tent. Who was going to catch Sarah when she fell?

Natalie knew the answer to that: her old friends. Her *always* friends. From Lakeview.

"I think we should try talking to Sarah again," Natalie said, sighing. "She just looks so sad and lonely."

"I agree, we all feel bad for her," Priya put in, "but come on. She spent all summer ignoring us and siding with Avery against us. And now that things have blown up in her face, it's not like she's come running back to us. It doesn't exactly seem like she's dying for our support, does it?"

"Things aren't always what they seem," Chelsea put in. "I mean, I should know. Sometimes you keep to yourself because you're afraid of being rejected. And Sarah is probably *really* embarrassed about what happened in the rec hall." She shot Avery an accusatory look, and Avery had the good grace to look ashamed of herself. "I think Natalie's right. I think we should give it another try. Sarah is one of our old-school crew—we owe it to her and to the Lakeview legacy not to give up so easily."

"What she said," Natalie said, smiling at one friend and making her way slowly toward another hopefully once and future friend at the same time. She beckoned to the group. "You all have to come with." Avery opened her mouth to protest, but Natalie cut her off with a wave of her hand. "Including you."

The girls marched off, Avery dutifully one pace behind.

Sarah looked up from her perch under the tree—she should have known what kind it was, after so many weeks of Walla Walla, but under the circumstances, she couldn't make herself care, it seemed—to find Natalie and the entire Oak tent crew wandering toward her looking purposeful. Great. Just what she needed. Another horrible reminder of all of the stupid mistakes she'd made since coming to Walla Walla. Awesome.

"We need to talk," Natalie said. Her voice was firm and insistent.

"I don't have anything to say," Sarah said, standing up and brushing grass off the backs of her legs. "I mean, nothing that's going to make any of this make sense for you guys."

"What happened, Sarah?" Natalie asked gently.

Sarah couldn't believe how patient Natalie sounded. How open. Even after everything that had gone down. She shook her head sadly as her eyes welled up again. "I don't know, honestly." She took a deep breath and decided to come clean. Now was as good a time as any—Joanna was there, and even Avery had joined the group, managing to look reasonably pleasant about it. Sarah didn't know what that was about, but she appreciated it, anyway. She sighed and started to talk.

"When I came to Walla Walla last year, I was terrified of starting over with a whole new group of girls. You guys know I'm shy, right?"

Natalie nodded encouragingly.

"So when Avery came up to me on the first day

of camp and asked me what my story was, I blanked. And the first thing that came into my mind was you, Natalie, and how *you* have this great, wild, crazy story. So I just . . . lied. I didn't mean to, I promise. It just popped out. But Avery was so impressed, and then everyone else ate it up, and . . . the whole thing just spiraled out of control."

"We understand," Jenna chimed in. "We've all been in situations where we didn't feel like we could be totally honest." She thought back to the summer when her parents had announced their divorce, and how she hadn't wanted to share her bad news with any of her friends. Of course, she had eventually learned that opening up can help to lighten a burden. She wanted Sarah to learn that, too.

"We've *all* been in situations like that," Natalie echoed. She glanced at Avery meaningfully. "Haven't we?"

Avery was silent.

Suddenly, the last person that Jenna would have expected to speak out, did.

It was Joanna. She stepped forward and elbowed Avery sharply in the ribs. "Avery," she prompted, don't you have something to say to Sarah?"

Avery shrugged. "Not really."

Now Joanna full-on pinched Avery on the shoulder. "Come *on*."

"*Ow!*" Avery shot Joanna a dirty look while Jenna stifled a giggle. "Fine."

"I'm sorry," Avery said quietly, looking at Sarah. "I'm sorry that I made you feel like you had to lie to impress me."

"And?" Joanna asked.

"And . . . it doesn't matter who your father is."

"And?" Joanna repeated, arching an eyebrow.

"And what?" Avery asked, exasperated. "What else is there?"

Joanna rolled her eyes. "I think there are some other people that you owe apologies to, also." She tilted her head toward Jenna and the rest of the group.

Avery sighed heavily. She looked up at the rest of the Lakeview girls. "Okay, fine. If you insist . . . I guess I really need to work on making new people feel at home."

At that, Natalie had to chuckle. "Understatement much?"

Avery nodded, taking it all in. "You hate me. I get it. I know I deserve it. But you have to understand—Walla Walla was my turf for so long, and when I heard that a bunch of new girls—who were all friends—were coming in together, I was afraid of how things were going to change."

"You were afraid?" Natalie asked, her voice high-pitched with disbelief. "How do you think we felt after we found out about the whole 'Outdoor CORE' thing?"

"Well, actually, I felt kind of good about it," Jenna reminded everyone, raising her hand.

"Oh my God, Jenna, can't you see that we're having a moment here!" Natalie teased her.

This small joke broke the tension. Everyone laughed and exchanged tentative looks.

"I was excited about having you guys here at camp," Sarah said, "but right away I realized that my secret was going to come out. I didn't know what to do. I had backed myself into a corner. The only solution was to keep you as far away from my friends as I possibly could."

"Hard to do when there's a huge game of Assassin going on," Natalie said, prompting a vigorous nod from Sarah.

"Yup. And I can't believe I won, too—the same night I was called out for being a big, fat liar." She laughed shortly. "Some winner. No one even wants to talk to me anymore."

"We're talking, aren't we?" Natalie pointed out. She moved to Sarah and put an arm around her shoulder, squeezing tight. "We're *all* talking. And that's the way it's going to be from now on." She looked at Avery with a challenge in her eyes.

"That is the way it's going to be from now on," Avery confirmed.

"In fact," Natalie went on, "we'll do you one better. Do you still have the final spoon from your triumphant victory?"

Sarah looked confused. "Yeah, but why? You want to go another round of Assassin?"

Natalie shook her head no. "Nah, that's enough cutthroat competition for yours truly. But I happen to have it on good authority that the kitchen staff stored a bunch of leftover ice cream and sundae toppings from the other night."

Sarah's eyes lit up. "Oooh! And there'll be

another staff meeting tonight, so we can sneak out after lights-out."

"I know all of the back paths," Avery reminded them. "I can get us to the mess hall and back without being spotted. That is—if you promise not to turn me in for sneaking out," she joked shyly.

"Honor code? What honor code?" Jenna grinned.

"We'll make our *own* Make Your Own Sundae night," Natalie confirmed. "That is, if you don't mind sharing your spoon with the rest of us."

"Of course I don't mind," Sarah said gratefully. "That's what friends are for!"

EPILOGUE

Dear Nicole,

It's been a whirlwind week here at Camp Walla Walla! Yes, yours truly DID win the game of Assassin. But for a while, it seemed as though I had lost just about everything else. I . . . told some lies in order to try and impress some people, and it finally caught up with me (it's a really long story, but I'll fill you in on all of the gory details when I get home.)

All of my old friends from

Lakeview who are here have been amazing and have given me another chance with them, even though I really don't deserve it. The Walla Walla originals, not so much, although they are slowly but surely starting to come around. Avery's been a lot more sensitive than I would have EVER thought she could be, I have to say—she even offered to speak to Josie and Tara about us swapping bunks so I could be with my old crew. But I decided to pass; there's no point in running away from my Walla Walla friends. I just have to deal with the fact that I kinda have to prove myself all over again. To everyone. My real self, this time. And anyway, I get to hang with my Lakeview buds every day. So it's not perfect, but we're getting there.

It's been a roller-coaster of a summer—and not at all what I expected when I signed up for camp again—but at the end of it all, if I can sort things out with everyone, then I get the best of both worlds, and even if I can't—well, it's a reunion with old friends, and finally, we're all having a blast—together!

Better late than never, right?

Miss you—can't wait to see you at school!

—Sarah

Turn the page for a sneak preview of

camp CONFIDENTIAL

Extra Credit

available now!

chapter
ONE

Posted by: Natalie
Subject: Who Wants to Be a Supahstah?

Or superstar if you're doing normal-speak.
Brynn, I can see you stretching your hand toward the
ceiling and me-me-me-ing even though I haven't given
any of the deets yet. Take a breath. Good. Now read on.
This director friend of my dad's is shooting a movie in
Guilford, CT and she needs a ton of middle-grade extras.
The movie is this time travel thriller where Sam Quinn is
searching for his lost son through all these different
time periods.

Some ammo for parents that need convincing.
The director has kids of her own, and is all about the
importance of school and bedtime and all that, so
she's only shooting the big scenes with all the extras on
weekends. If you want in, all you gotta do is show up
at 8943 Stockton Ave two weeks from Saturday at 10.

Love you! Mean it!
Nat

Natalie was so glad the Camp Lakeview blog hadn't shut down when the camp had. It had just kind of morphed into the Lakeviewalla blog. Mostly Lakeview girls—make that former-Lakeview-now-Walla-Walla girls—but with a few old-time Camp Walla Walla girls mixed in. Like Avery, who had been one of Natalie, Jenna, Sloan, Chelsea, and Priya's tentmates over the summer.

For most of the summer, it had seemed like there was absolutely nothing in Avery to like, but she'd turned out to have a hidden streak of actual niceness. Living with her reminded Natalie of the first summer with Chelsea. And Chelsea had ended up a friend too.

If Avery decided she wanted to be an extra, it would actually be sort of cool. Natalie was almost positive she could count on getting in some Brynn time. She figured Brynn would do anything to get her parents' permission to be in the movie—hunger strike, non-stop Shakespeare recitations at full volume. She might even get one of her drama club girls to impersonate her while she snuck off to Connecticut. Natalie smiled at the thought of Brynn coaching someone to act like her. Impossible. There was nobody quite like Brynn.

Posted by: Brynn
Subject: . . .

. . . .
That's me being speechless. You guys, I'm speechless. Have you ever seen—I mean heard—me

speechless before? I don't think so. But when I read
Nat's email, my voice got sucked right out of me.
Seriously, I had to drink a glass of grapefruit juice—
which, ewww—to remoisturize my mouth so I could ask
my parents if I could be a Supahstah. They weren't
thrilled with me commuting 2 ½ hours to Guilford,
but I told them I could use the train time for homework,
and now I'm going to be in a movie! Yes, yes, yes! Yes!
Promise I'll remember I knew you when.

Brynn

Posted by: Sarah
Subject: McSwoony

Sam Quinn is in the movie. Sam. Quinn. I am so there.

Sars

Posted by: Jenna
Subject: McOldy

Sarah, it must be said. Sam Quinn is old. Can't
wait to see my Walla Walla/Lakeview girls on the big
screen!

Jenna

Posted by: Brynn
Subject: Thinkless

I was thinkless as well as speechless when I posted

before. I forgot to ask who else is going to join me in stardom? Nat, you're going to be in the movie, right? NYC is closer to Guilford than Boston is.

What about you, Pree? We could meet up on the train. I know drama isn't especially your thing, but it'll be fu-uhn being an extra. Avery? You're right in Connecticut? You in?

Sarah, no swooning over McSwoony. Being an extra is a professional gig! (Well, you can swoon on the inside.)

B

Posted by: Priya
Subject: Bike Marathon

Jordan and I entered this bike marathon. It's not for a month and a half, but I have to train. There is no way that boy is beating me.

This will probably be my last post for a month and a half. Talk to you all after I kick behind!

Priya

Posted by: Brynn
Subject: Jordan's behind

No kicking, Pree! I like my b.f.'s behind the way it is!

Posted by: Sloan
Subject: Outlook Good

I've consulted the Tarot, the I Ching, the leaves in the cup of tea I just drank, and, of course, the Magic Eight Ball. All revealed a happy outcome for the extras in the movie. Go for it! The Sedona Girl knows all.

Luv,
Sloan

Natalie grinned as she read Sloan's post. Of course being an extra was going to be a happy outcome. Natalie wasn't a drama girl like Brynn or a Sam Quinn megafan like Sarah, but hanging out on a movie set with her buds—what could be bad?

Posted by: Natalie
Subject: Outlook Fantabulous

I'm not from Sedona, center of all things mystical. But I am from NYC, and New Yorkers know everything. I say the outlook for the extras is more than good. It's good squared. (See, I know math. Told you NYC-ers know it all!)

Can't wait to see some of my camp girls in a couple weeks!!

J'adore! (I know French too! Well, perfume French.)

Natalie